ANDREW DORAN
AND THE
SCROLL OF
NIGHTMARES

BY MATTHEW DAVENPORT

"He's a version of me from a universe very similar to ours," I explained.

Nancy couldn't take her eyes off my duplicate. "Why does he look different?"

The other me answered, "There are many different universes. Some of those are almost the same as the universe you're in. Except for one or two differences." He nodded to my hand that was intact and not withered like his own. "I'm guessing you either haven't time-traveled, or you've learned how to hide from the Hounds of Tindalos."

I shook my head. "No time travel, yet."

"Why am I here?" he asked.

"I tripped a trap," I said, nodding toward the golden threads. Already, more people were stepping from the stone walls and breaking the last of the gold lines. "For some reason, the trap pulls different versions of whoever stepped into it."

Nancy frowned. "How would that be a successful trap?"

"Well," I ventured a guess, "we haven't moved forward yet." I turned my attention to my transdimensional copy. "What were you doing before you showed up here?"

He couldn't take his eyes from the newly appearing versions of myself. There were seven more Andrew Dorans all trying to figure out where they had ended up. That wasn't entirely correct, as one of the Dorans was actually my little sister, Mary Doran, wearing my standard utilitarian style. The rest were also wearing similar clothes to mine, but with differing scars, hats, facial hair, and weaponry. One of them even had a bullwhip, as if that could be useful.

Caves of Namibia

The cave that I entered wasn't well known to the locals and if it weren't for the combined efforts of my traveling companion and my administrative assistant, it would have remained unknown to me as well.

I was in Namibia, hopefully on the trail of the original Book of Eibon. Nancy Dyer, my friend and assistant in my travels, had been attempting to decipher the location of the historic tome from her dead father's journal. All that she could figure out was that the Book of Eibon was located somewhere in southern Africa and possibly in a pyramid. In my years of education in anthropology, I was aware of no pyramids in the southern half of Africa. Applying that knowledge to Nancy's translation brought the realization that we were looking for a tomb, and not a pyramid.

That was when my secretary at Miskatonic University, Carol Berg, made a comment that solved the mystery for us.

Carol Berg is one of the few domesticated wendigo in existence. Wendigo are beasts born of eating human flesh. They are fast and vicious killers, but they get their power from an alien god of survival.

Nancy and Carol had been deep into their research, with no clue as to their next turn, when Carol mumbled, "Ithaqua help us."

My attention only barely caught it, but that was enough to trigger a series of historical and occult facts regarding Ithaqua. His home was Hyperborea, a legendary land of constant daylight, dry climates, and formidable winter conditions. While many people thought that Hyperborea was an old name for Greenland, anyone who had read the numerous occult and alien texts that I subjected myself to knew that Hyperborea was another world.

Another world accessible through portals in our world.

Portals originally hidden in caves.

Hyperborea was also where a dark wizard named Eibon wrote a certain book that would be poorly translated and horribly copied many times.

That was the break we needed to start our hunt for caves that led to Hyperborea in southern Africa. The search wasn't easy, as the only previously mapped portals to the alien world were only known to exist in Greenland.

This was the fifth cave I had checked and only the second in Namibia. Each of the caves were potentials on our list because they had been referenced in the Necronomicon as gateways to other worlds.

Namibia is a warm and dry place, but as soon as I entered the cave I was hit by a cool breeze. The walls were rough stone for a hundred meters or so as I climbed deeper into the Earth. After that, they changed in texture and color, becoming smooth and black like obsidian. They shifted from organic round tunnels cut through the stone by natural processes to square halls made by some intelligent design.

Nancy was encouraged by the shift and began charging forward, the beam of her flashlight bouncing around as she ran. I grabbed her arm as she made to dart past me.

"What are you doing?" she asked. "This has to be it."

I nodded. "I agree, but running into a cave that has successfully protected the Book of Eibon for thousands of years might get us killed." Lowering my voice, I added, "Eibon was a wizard. I hate wizards."

Nancy frowned. "You think there are traps?"

She was a beautiful woman in her mid-twenties with short, blond hair. She was dressed much as I was, in a buttoned shirt and tan trousers. Both her father, William Dyer, and my friend, Leo Dubois, died as we fought Nazi soldiers in an ancient alien city in Antarctica. Having lost my friend and assistant and with Nancy wanting to learn more about the aspects of the world that had estranged her from her father, she took Leo's job as my gun-toting assistant.

"You don't?" I countered. "I'm less concerned with if there are traps and more concerned with what style of traps there are."

We both took our flashlights and began aiming them at the walls, the floor, and the ceiling. I stepped ahead of Nancy and led the way forward. It wasn't for any sort of masculine reason, as Nancy had shown over and over again that she was more than capable of holding her own in any situation. I took the lead because I was more familiar with the types of traps that might exist from alien worlds.

Opening my senses, I sought the power that leaked from the veil that separated our world and the next. I whispered a spell that I had learned from Haitian worshipers of Hastur. "Shglatn."

In the hopes of saving my sanity, I had long ago chosen not to learn the language of Hastur and didn't know what the word actually meant, but I knew what the spell was used for. It was meant to reveal things that had been purposefully hidden.

The word left my lips and carried with it a golden energy that radiated outward and down the dark corridor.

Nancy let out a gasp and gripped my arm as she pointed at the ground. About ten meters in front of us was a golden patch in the floor. The gold was the spell showing us a hidden trap. I pulled a coin from my pocket and tossed it at the spot on the floor. It stopped and floated above the spot on the floor.

I moved closer to examine the floating coin. As I squatted in front of it, Nancy came forward and pressed her gun toward the coin. She was carrying a Thomson submachine gun. The tip of the Tommy gun went through the invisible field easily enough. When it touched the coin, the coin was suddenly overcome by gravity and began its descent. When gravity forced it to break contact with Nancy's gun, the coin froze in the air again.

"How does that work?" Nancy whispered.

I pulled out my Non-Commissioned Cavalry sword. The blade was as black as the walls surrounding us and covered in carved runes. The weapon was a powerful deterrent against the powers and beings that crossed into our world from beyond the veil, but that wasn't what I needed it for. I turned the blade flat and slid it through the magical field directly under the coin. Once it was through the field and the first few inches of the tip were through the other side of the field, I raised the sword until it touched the underside of the coin.

The coin's fall continued with it landing on the flat of the blade. I slid the sword forward and back before retrieving and pocketing the coin.

"This is the first trap," I explained. "It freezes time, but only for objects that are entirely in the field. The field is small enough that if you're aware of it being there you can stretch your arms out and walk, and you'll be able to keep a part of yourself outside the field."

Nancy sighed. "So, if we didn't know that the trap was there ..."

I nodded. "We would have walked into it and been frozen in place until we either died or someone pushed us through."

Nancy slung the strap of the machine gun over her neck and spread her arms to each side. I did the same thing and said, "I'll go first."

"I don't think so," Nancy exclaimed. "If you're wrong and you get stuck in there, how am I supposed to get you out? You at least know magic and things that could help." She crooked her thumb at herself. "I'll go first, and if I get stuck you can spend the rest of your life trying to unstick me."

I smirked and bowed toward the still faintly glowing section of the floor. "After you."

She grabbed my hand to anchor herself to me outside the field. Nancy held her breath as she stepped forward, side-stepping into the invisible field. Her other hand crossed the barrier without any resistance. She continued forward, scrunching up her face as she went more fully into the field. When her hand exited where I figured the other side of the field was, I relaxed only slightly. This had all been a theory until Nancy had pressed through and into the other side. When it was my turn, my grip tightened on Nancy's and I also held my breath.

Once we were both on the other side, I started forward, my excitement renewed. I was five steps away from the previous trap when I heard a click and came to a halt. Cursing myself, I realized that I had just done what I previously chastised Nancy for doing. I whispered "Shglatn" again and watched as invisible threads were highlighted in golden light. They crisscrossed the tunnel ahead of us. I looked down and saw that one was going through my chest.

That gave me some information. These weren't physical objects in our reality. That was all I had though. These could be putting in or taking something from my life. I had no idea what this trap consisted of.

"Well?" Nancy asked from behind me. "You probably shouldn't have been rushing ahead. There might be traps here."

"Not helping," I shot back.

"What now?" Nancy was looking closely at the strands, being careful not to touch them.

I let out a slow sigh and noticed that as my chest moved the string wasn't affected. "At this point," I said slowly so as to not trigger the trap sooner, "my only option is to trip the trap."

Nancy didn't say anything as she backed away as far as she could without stepping into the time field of the previous trap.

I stepped back and watched as the glowing thread of whatever it was passed from my body. The thread that had touched me suddenly snapped out of existence, the golden energy of my spell making it look like a long bubble popping.

For a moment, we weren't sure that I had tripped the trap. Nancy and I shot each other curious looks until we heard a noise.

Stepping out of the wall on the right, near where the thread had been touching, was a man. He coalesced from the stone, forming into a fully dressed and ruggedly handsome man.

It was me.

Except that it wasn't at the same time. He was clean shaven and instead of my usual sword and pistol, he carried a machine gun covered in runes. His left hand was withered and blackened with some sort of decay.

"Is that you?" Nancy was staring at the man, but I couldn't

get over the fact that as he appeared out of the wall, he broke more of the threads of the trap.

"No," my doppelganger and I said at the same time.

"He's a version of me from a universe very similar to ours," I explained.

Nancy couldn't take her eyes off my duplicate. "Why does he look different?"

The other me answered, "There are many different universes. Some of those are almost the same as the universe you're in. Except for one or two differences." He nodded to my hand that was intact and not withered like his own. "I'm guessing you either haven't time-traveled, or you've learned how to hide from the Hounds of Tindalos."

I shook my head. "No time travel, yet."

"Why am I here?" he asked.

"I tripped a trap," I said, nodding toward the golden threads. Already, more people were stepping from the stone walls and breaking the last of the gold lines. "For some reason, the trap pulls different versions of whoever stepped into it."

Nancy frowned. "How would that be a successful trap?"

"Well," I ventured a guess, "we haven't moved forward yet." I turned my attention to my transdimensional copy. "What were you doing before you showed up here?"

He couldn't take his eyes from the newly appearing versions of myself. There were seven more Andrew Dorans all trying to figure out where they had ended up. That wasn't entirely correct, as one of the Dorans was actually my little sister, Mary Doran, wearing my standard utilitarian style. The rest were also wearing similar clothes to mine, but with differing scars, hats, facial hair, and weaponry. One of them even had a bullwhip, as if that could be useful.

The first one that had appeared was staring at one farthest from us. I saw him as well.

His eyes were entirely black, and it was obvious that it wasn't my mind that resided in that body.

"I was hunting for the Book of Eibon," he answered under his breath. "Have you had the dream?"

I nodded, recognizing the last one for what he was. "Yes.

It would make sense that there was a universe where it came true."

My copy drew his machine gun, and the other versions of me all drew their weapons as well, each of them attempting to take aim, but the confusion of the scenario making it difficult who to aim at.

"All right." Nancy ducked as low as she could, bringing up her tommy gun as she did. "I get it now. This is a great trap."

I was reacting no better than any of my counterparts, aiming my gun at the version of me farthest away. Some of the other Dorans had seen him and obviously turned their guns on him as well.

When the Nazi-controlled psychic warriors known as the Traum Kult had stolen the American version of the Necronomicon, I had been put into a dream state and shown a potential future. In this prophecy, I watched as a seemingly possessed version of myself stood upon a shore covered with squirming masses of oily black flesh. Psychic pressure built in my head as the evil Doran chanted a spell meant to bring forth a monstrous entity. He was chanting the call that would awaken Cthulhu from his sunken house in R'yleh.

Waking from the prophecy changed everything. Not only was I hellbent on making certain that the prophecy never came true, but I was marked by cultists of Cthulhu, and those who knew of the prophecy, as the Bringer of Cthulhu. I was his chosen herald and I'd destroyed the Necronomicon to save the world and myself from that fate.

The dark version of me in the sea of Dorans was from a universe in which I had taken up that mantle and worn it proudly. This was the Bringer of Cthulhu.

He barked a magical phrase that I had never heard before, and a wave of power threw all of us back. Nancy bounced into the time field, freezing in the middle of her fall. The two Andrews closest to the blast were destroyed, disintegrating as raw power echoed from the Bringer's mouth.

I had expected some sort of attack and managed to brace myself and avoid Nancy's fate. The mistake that my counterparts were likely to make, as it was one that I almost made, was in assuming that our attacker was another Andrew Doran. He was a monster wearing my face and I'd dealt with a few of those before. This wasn't a fight I could win, but it might be a fight that I could end.

I opened my senses to the power behind the veil and saw all of my counterparts in an entirely new light. They were all still tethered to their own realities and the powers they would have tapped into from there. Aside from the slight shift in their different colors, as my brain interpreted it, from their worlds, each of them had the magical scarring that I was certain I would see on my own self if I could ever turn that vision onto myself. Mary's energy was the purest and strongest of the bunch. My sister's doppelganger had a magical potential that was much stronger than anything I had ever tried to wield. That was interesting to know.

The Andrew closest to me, with the withered hand, was entirely lacking his hand on the spiritual plane. It looked like time travel had a dangerous cost and the Hounds of Tindalos took more than their pound of flesh.

The Bringer was a black mass of wiggling, oily flesh. Nothing remained of the Andrew whose place he had taken. He existed entirely to serve the alien god.

I pushed my observations away and used my limited magical abilities to pluck at the differences in each of my duplicates, starting with the Bringer. The result was each of them briefly flashing out of our reality, indicating that I was on the right path.

Noticing what I was attempting to do, the Bringer opened his mouth to send forth another wave of energy.

Before he could release the power that he was summoning, I reached out and pulled on each of them again with the power of my reality's thin veil between worlds.

There was a wet popping noise and each of them were gone.

The Bringer had returned to terrorize his world.

I holstered my magical pistol and turned to Nancy's frozen form. Reaching through the field of invisible energy, I grasped her wrist, connecting her to the progressive flow of time. Gravity regained control over her and she gasped as she fell. I didn't let up my grip or allow my assistant to pull me into the field. Instead, I pulled her forward and out of the field.

"Where'd they go?" Nancy had pulled herself out of my grip and brought up her machine gun in one fluid motion.

"Gone," I answered. "Whatever magic that trap had used to pull them here wasn't meant to be permanent. I found the tethers holding them to their respective worlds and pulled on them."

Nancy stared into my eyes, obviously looking for something that wasn't there. "Even the mean one?"

"Yes." I decided no other explanation was necessary.

"What was his story? And the lady one, who was that?" Nancy wasn't willing to let it drop. "And what's a Hound of Tin … um … Tinda—"

"Hound of Tindalos," I finished for her. "They are a type of demon creature that hunt down and devour time travelers."

"Like my father?" Nancy's voice had a hint of fear, but she'd never show it.

I shook my head. "Your father's mind time-traveled. The Hounds hunt people who discover how to travel with their bodies." I sighed and stepped forward, whispering my Haitian magic again to see if the trap had reset. It hadn't. "As for the lady, that was my sister, Mary. Wherever she came from was a place that had seen her take up the quest for the Book of Eibon instead of me." I didn't add that it also implied that she had basically taken up my entire fight against the occult, as that's what led Nancy and me down to these caves. "I don't know what the story was with the black-eyed version of me."

I didn't like lying to Nancy, but she didn't need to know about the prophecy. Not yet, anyway. There were enough things in this reality to fear without making her question her allies.

"Whatever road he took was a much darker one than I am on," I added to squash any remaining fears she might have of his incredible destructive powers. "I'm not him."

Nancy nodded. "Obviously. He probably wouldn't have walked into that trap." She snickered to herself. "As a matter of fact, none of them walked into that trap or you would have been pulled into their realities. So," she hit my arm playfully, "you're the dumbest one."

I couldn't help but laugh. "Fair enough."

We marched farther down the tunnel and deeper into the Earth. I continued to whisper "Shglatn" as we continued, keeping ever vigilant in my search for more of the ancient wizard's traps.

While wizards were historically and fictionally known for their clever traps, the things present in this cave were beyond any magic that I had previously thought humans capable of wielding. It made it impossible to predict when and where the next trap would appear and made for slow progress. These were Hyperborean spells from that other world.

The air chilled around us as we turned another corner. Wind filled the corridor, and the breeze carried on it the smell of winter.

Nancy shivered. "I didn't expect the temperature shift."

I jumped twice before I answered. "The gravity is different, too. I think we've crossed over from our world to Hyperborea."

"We're on another planet?" Nancy's eyes went wide with a mix of excitement and fear. "What if we get stuck here?"

I shook my head. "I don't think that we can. The worlds are tethered together through a few caves like this. If for some reason this cave became closed off to us, we could travel through Hyperborea until we found another cave."

We continued forward until we entered a large cavern. My Haitian spell didn't reveal a trap, but there's much to be said about intuition. The room was almost perfectly round. It was like a large cake tin of black stone. The smell of death struck my nose and I raised my light. The floor was littered with corpses. As the light fell on them, we could see corpses that were obviously centuries old and consisted of nothing more than bones and dust, but also corpses as new as the two closest to us. They were German soldiers and they looked like recent deaths.

"This doesn't bode well." I was only barely audible, but the sound of my voice echoed back to us from across the cavern. It was disconcerting to say the least. "Why am I always crawling into caves filled with death?"

Nancy shrugged and stepped forward, past the first few corpses. "Everyone needs a hobby."

I started to follow Nancy, but after I stepped into the cylindrical cave there was a light pop as the pressure in the room changed. I spun around as Nancy shined her light ahead of her.

In unison we said, "The door is gone."

The entrance and exit to the cavern had been replaced by solid stone. It looked as if they had never been there.

"They're moving," Nancy said, her voice reaching an unexpected pitch as she backed into me. I spun around, pointing my flashlight as the bodies around us, even the ones without muscle tissue, began climbing to their feet.

"Get behind me." I drew my sword. The runes carved into its blade glowed with an unnatural light. Holding it in one hand, and the flashlight in the other, I added, "Don't use your gun unless you want to go deaf."

Nancy nodded before fear popped into her head. "What am I supposed to do if you get overwhelmed?"

I withdrew a knife that had the crude symbol of the Al-Azif, the original "first draft" of the Necronomicon, carved into its blade. I had acquired the knife from a hermit in the Adirondack Mountains of upstate New York when we had hunted down cultists in search of my missing sister. We managed to save my sister and the hermit had let me keep his hunting knife. "Use this. It should be able to put them down permanently." I didn't add that I had never tried it against creatures not born of the Al-Azif, but Nancy needed confidence, not doubt.

The first corpse to reach me was a skeleton that was only barely held together, and by what, I did not know. As it lunged at me, I cut off its head with my sword. The moment that my blade touched it, the skeleton fell to the cavern floor.

A gasp from Nancy caused me to spin to see what grabbed her attention. Behind us, the two Nazi soldiers had climbed to their feet and rushed us. Nancy knocked the first one toward me with the butt of her machine gun and I ran him through with my sword. The second dead German dove at me, but I still had my sword in his companion. I planted my boot on the impaled German's chest and kicked him off the sword and onto his friend. The resulting momentum backward pushed me into two older corpses that I hadn't seen. They grabbed and clawed at my clothing, but I swung my sword over my head and around me in an arc that knocked them both off me and cut them enough that the blade's magic dropped them.

When I returned my attention to the second Nazi undead, it was to see Nancy wrestling with him. She had jammed the knife I had given her into the German's temple and was hanging on to it as the beast thrashed wildly. Holding that blade was the only thing that kept the monster's teeth away from Nancy's flesh.

I lunged forward and placed the tip of my sword through the side of his neck. If he had been alive, his jugular would have exploded with blood. Instead, he collapsed on top of my assistant.

I helped Nancy out from under the twice-dead soldier and tried to ignore her glare.

"I thought you said the knife would kill them?" The venom in her voice was hard to miss.

My blade cut through two more of the oncoming corpses before I answered. "Well, I hoped that it would, but I wasn't certain."

As the last corpse fell, the passageways returned, popping back into existence.

"Here's your useless knife back." Nancy handed me the knife.

"It's not useless," I explained. "It's fatal to creatures of the Al-Azif."

Nancy looked around her. "Are these creatures of the Al-Azif?" I shook my head. "Then that knife is useless," she barked, and I couldn't help but agree with her logic as I slid the blade back into its sheath on my belt.

The passage out of the cavern continued for about ten meters before we came across a pedestal with a sheet of ancient-looking parchment lying on top of it. Looking at the parchment with my flashlight made my head hurt; the letters seemed to dance across the page and shift with the angle of the light. Alien words and ancient magic had that effect on the mortal mind. Grabbing the parchment, I half expected another trap to trip and cursed myself for not whispering my trap-revealing spell.

When nothing triggered, I slid the parchment into my satchel and had a sudden, concerning thought. I drew my pistol from its holster and placed it in the satchel with the ancient paper.

"Why did you do that?" Nancy asked.

"Old habits," I explained. "Whenever I think I've got what I've come for, someone always wants to take it away. It might be a good idea to keep the pistol near it."

Nancy didn't question my actions further but nodded to the satchel. "It doesn't look like much of a book."

It had only been one sheet of paper, but my assistant wasn't wrong. "The Book of Eibon is the title of many copies of this text, but I'm beginning to think that those aren't titles so much as poor translations or spell books of another sort disguised as the Book of Eibon." I patted the satchel. "The windswept and frozen planes of Hyperborea aren't the place for a book, but maybe they are the place for a scroll of his most important spells." I didn't add what I was really thinking, though.

That we knew absolutely nothing about what that old wizard had decided was important enough to write down.

We made our way back through the caves and the traps. We expected the cavern of corpses to reanimate but were pleasantly surprised when they didn't. Earth's gravity returned and hit both of us with a gasp. During our short time on Hyperborea, we had become accustomed to the lighter gravity. That being said, the added weight to our bodies was a comfort as we realized we were back on our home planet.

The web of different existences hadn't been rearmed and the time prison was gone. It seemed that the piece of parchment on the pedestal had been holding each of these traps in place and removing it disarmed them.

Along with the increase in gravity, we had also been greeted by the arid air of Namibia which only got worse as we stepped out of the cave and into daylight.

The cave had been a little over ten kilometers west of Namibia's largest city, Windhoek. With Namibia's strong ties to Germany, we had done our best to keep a low profile in Windhoek as we searched for the caves. While the city had been more or less liberated by the German occupation during the first global conflict of this century, they still had sympathizers, and the last thing that Nancy and I needed was for the Nazis to know that we were in the area.

Unfortunately, we hadn't covered our trails well enough.

Nancy was the first one out of the cave and I came up behind her, blinded by the sun as my eyes adjusted. Nancy gave me a swift elbow to the ribs, and I was about to chastise her when I saw that she was directing my attention to the sixteen German soldiers standing in front of us.

I raised my hands and straightened my back, squinting against the sun.

One soldier, a Generaloberst, the equivalent of an American General, stepped forward with his hands behind his back as his men raised their rifles at Nancy and me.

"Hello, Dr. Doran." His accent was less pronounced than most of the Nazis I've had to deal with. "I am Wolfhard Schildenfeld of the Ahnenerbe."

"The what?" Nancy asked.

A snort of derision escaped me as I answered Nancy. "The Ahnenerbe are Heinrich Himmler's occult archaeologists. They search for historical truth to the rule of the Aryan race. At least they used to, until Himmler began directing them to search for occult artifacts to help the Fuehrer win the war." I laughed. "They're Germany's cultist army."

Nancy smiled as I derided the soldier in front of us.

Schildenfeld forced a tight-lipped smile. "When my two men failed to return from the caves, I made my remaining men pull back and wait for you. Why waste good men when the famous Andrew Doran could do the work for us?" He held out his hand to Nancy and me. "Now, if you don't mind, please hand over the Book of Eibon and perhaps we won't—" he stopped in the middle of his demand.

"Won't what?" I asked, genuinely curious.

Nancy jabbed me in the ribs again.

"Would you stop that?" I demanded before noticing where her attention was.

All of the German soldiers were frozen in place. Schildenfeld hadn't stopped talking for any sort of dramatic effect. Something had caused the Nazis to halt in their positions. Whatever it was wasn't like the time spell we had run into in the caves, but instead was something cast directly on their minds. Several of the soldiers had already started to bleed from their eyes under the psychic pressure that was being put upon them.

From behind the soldiers came five people wearing dark red robes with a golden symbol on their chests. The symbol was the outline of a head with an eye in the center. Three of the cultists approaching us had their hands held high and in the direction of the Germans. They were the ones casting the psychic spell.

Their leader approached me and lowered her hood.

"Doctor, please ignore them and give me the Book of Eibon." As she said it, she brushed her hand through her blond hair, revealing dark eyes and high cheekbones.

Nancy's confusion was clear on her face. "And who are you?"

"She's Anita Blumenthal," I explained. "Formerly of the Nazi-sympathizing group of ancient psychic warriors known as the Traum Kult." I leaned in and said to Nancy, "That's 'Dream Cult' in German."

Nancy rolled her eyes. "Thanks."

I turned my attention to Anita. "Didn't I destroy your book club?" I nodded to the emblem on her robe. "Shouldn't you all be in hiding or something?"

Though previously controlled by Heinrich Himmler himself, most of the Traum Kult weren't actually German, having recruited their members from all corners of the world. Anita replied in the thick English accent of her birth. "A man of your reputation should know to make certain an enemy is dead before leaving it wounded and alone. We have reformed, stronger than ever." She turned to indicate her fellow cultists. "When you destroyed our leadership, we had a sudden realization that working for our German overseers was stifling our," she gave a small laugh, "creativity. When we reformed, we disavowed our ties to any governments and have since returned to our roots."

"As underground collectors of the occult and assassins for hire?" I asked.

"A crass explanation," Anita said with a sigh, "but not inaccurate."

One of the German soldiers collapsed, dead from the strain on his mind.

"I'd love to stick around and talk your ear off, but as much as I love seeing Nazis die, my assistant and I really should get going." I made to step around Nancy as if to leave, but knew that wasn't in the cards. In reality, my move had been to place myself between my assistant with the machine gun and the psychic warrior. If this was going to turn into a fight, I would rather Anita aim her mental powers at me, someone who might be able to fend her off, while Nancy cut her down with bullets.

"No," Anita's voice echoed through my head. "You will give me the Book of Eibon, now."

I sighed, threw Nancy a quick glance, and said, "See what I mean about old habits?" Reaching into the satchel, I placed my hand on the grip of my magical revolver.

No sooner than my hand had tightened on the grip, her nearest cultist lackey gave a shout.

"Get down!"

My momentary surprise at having been discovered was quickly replaced by confusion as the sound of a vehicle hit my ears followed by a volley of gunfire. I grabbed Nancy and dove back into the cover of the cave as bullets tore through frozen Nazis and unprepared cultists. As the cultists fell or lost their concentration, the Nazis regained their ability to move. Within seconds of our landing in the cave, Generaloberst Wolfhard Schildenfeld was shouting for his men to return fire. Nancy raised her machine gun and started out of the cave, but I grabbed her arm.

"There are three groups out there shooting at each other." I nodded at the machine gun. "Don't you think we should sit this one out and let them kill each other?"

Never one to stand down from a fight, Nancy struggled with the idea, but settled on not advancing. Instead, we kept just inside the cover of the cave entrance and waited to make our move.

What I could see didn't really tell me much. A large jeep

had driven close by and parked. There were two men with their heads wrapped in cloth, but the rest of their bodies dressed in unmarked military fatigues in the matching green of the United States Army. Supposedly from the jeep, they were walking away from the vehicle and using machine guns to cut away at the cultists and Germans. The Traum Kult and the Nazis weren't helping themselves any as they continued to take shots at each other as the two well-armed men advanced. They had cut a path between us and them before the one closest to us began shouting.

"Dr. Doran and Nancy Dyer, please make your way to the vehicles as quickly as you can."

I gave Nancy a look to see how she felt about that idea, but instead of returning a look that might answer my curiosity, she took off out of the cave and toward the jeep.

That decision apparently made, I followed her. We jumped into the vehicle to find a third man wearing a similar headdress and fatigues, sitting behind the wheel. We waited just long enough for the driver's companions to return to the vehicle before we took off into the Namibia desert.

Debriefed

Gunfire raked the back of our saviors' vehicle, causing me to instinctively dive forward and cover my head. I was only in that position for a moment before the explosive echo of Nancy's machine gun joined the returning fire of the men riding with us. Nancy's reflexes had taken a different turn than mine had, and she had spun around in her seat to fire on our pursuers.

The gunfire from both sides died down quicker than I had anticipated. A quick glance out the back window showed me that the fight between the Traum Kult and the Germans had escalated as the Germans fought animated golems of stone. With their hands full, they couldn't go after us immediately.

I settled down in the back seat of the jeep. It was cramped with both Nancy and me, and the third gunman. He lowered the cloth around his head to show a rugged face of stubble and grit. He kept casting glances toward the fight that we'd just left but lowered his machine gun to his lap.

He turned forward and tapped the driver on the shoulder. "We're clear. Head to the pick-up."

"The pick-up?" I asked. He gave me a look as if noticing me for the first time. "I don't mean to sound ungrateful," I aimed my pistol at the driver, "but could you tell us who you are? We've had enough of people trying to kidnap or kill us."

Nancy reached forward and pressed her hand on top of the pistol, forcing me to bring it down, but I didn't take my finger off the trigger.

The passenger in the front seat twisted around and thrust his hand toward me. As he lowered his own face covering and stuck out his hand, I realized he had darker skin and was missing a finger on his right hand.

"Dr. Doran, my name is Sergeant Harvey Neil of the United States." He pointed at the driver and then the man sitting next to us. "This is Jack and that's Private Tim Ruddel. My men and I were tasked with keeping an eye on you once you entered Namibia." I put away my pistol and shook his hand. When I let go, he waved in the direction of the skirmish behind us. "It became obvious that we would need to extract you when we saw the Germans taking up position." Harvey let out a whistle. "We didn't expect the Traum Kult, though. That was a surprise."

"And you know who the Traum Kult are?" His free use of the name made the answer obvious, but the Traum Kult were a secret society of psychic assassins. Why he was aware of the Traum Kult was beyond me.

Harvey turned more in his seat so that he could see me more clearly.

"Dr. Doran, have you ever heard of the United States Esoteric Cavalry?"

The question tickled a memory in the back of my mind, and I glanced down at my sword in its scabbard, uncomfortably wedged between myself and the door of the jeep. During my last adventure, Nancy had told me that she was aware of the unique history regarding my magical .38 revolver. We had yet to have that conversation, but it flooded me with curiosity regarding my other weapon of choice, the 1840 Non-Commissioned Officer's sword. I had never seen anything like it before returning to Miskatonic. The hilt was standard for the type of sword, but the blade was made out of a black metal with runes directly from the pages of the Necronomicon etched into the blade. I had yet to find a single creature with connections to the void that didn't suffer intense pain when it came into contact with the blade.

"Yes," Harvey noticed my glance to the blade. "That sword was forged for Captain Arlington Fitz the day that the United States Esoteric Cavalry was formed. We're a secret branch of the United States Military that operates in much the same way that you do, but in groups." He nodded toward "Jack," whose lack of a surname and having not removed his own fabric from his face made me wonder who he really was. "We helped your university begin filling its armory and have secretly fought the Traum Kult and the Ahnenerbe for years."

"You're after the Book of Eibon, too?" Nancy asked with a hint of irritation in her voice. The book had been hinted at in her father's journal as a dangerous item not meant for mortal hands. She saw it as her own personal duty to make certain that it remained out of the reach of those who would abuse it. I watched as she tightened her grip on her tommy gun.

"That's not our current assignment," Sergeant Neil said. "Our mission is to get you back to the United States the minute that you have the Book of Eibon in your possession." He returned to facing forward and looking out the window. "Once you've been debriefed, we're to take you and the book back to Miskatonic University."

"What does the debriefing consist of?" I asked.

"Questions regarding your discovery of the portal to Hyperborea and anything that you might have encountered in the cave." He paused for just a moment before adding, "The USEC is aware of the existence of other worlds. We've been fighting it back for generations, but we're concerned that something bigger is coming and we need to be prepared. There are some people that believe that you and that shithole of a town that you come from are going to be pivotal in that preparation."

"What do you believe?" Nancy caught the same hint of derision in his voice that I had.

"What I think doesn't matter," was the answer he gave, but he quickly added, "but if it did, I'd have had my men execute your friend here. I've heard just as many theories that Andrew Doran will bring on the end of the world as I've heard that he'll save it." Harvey shifted his attention to me. "The way I understand these things, you can't be as deep in the shit as you are, Doran, without getting covered in the stuff."

"Says the guy who knows more about my magical sword than I do," I countered.

Rage filled Harvey's voice, "That sword is a legacy that should never have been donated to your twisted museum. We're fighting a war on two fronts and while your recent efforts have made the government more interested in working with

Miskatonic University, some of us won't ever forget that most of the problems currently facing us on at least one of those fronts stem from that damned school."

"Why don't we all calm down just a minute," Nancy piped up. She threw me a glance that told me to keep my mouth shut. "We appreciate you stepping in, but neither of us works for the government. We don't need to cooperate with a debriefing."

Tim gave a small laugh from Nancy's left. "Calling it a debriefing is Sarge's polite way of asking you to cooperate. Otherwise, we could call it an interrogation."

"We aren't being arrested?" Nancy pressed.

Tim shook his head. "Whether you cooperate or not, we've been given orders to release you once we have any and all information that you can provide."

I looked out the window and watched as small tufts of grass and short trees passed by. I could just make out a zebra in the distance. Namibia's arid climate wasn't conducive to a lot of plant growth, but they had beautiful animals. It was a reminder that this world wasn't just a beacon for the horrible, but also home to beauty, as well.

"Alright," I said, implying that I had a choice. "We'll cooperate, but the first thing I need to know is what's going on with 'Jack'?"

Jack's head lifted only slightly at the mention of his name.

Harvey hesitated before saying, "What makes you think there's anything going on with him?"

"Like you said," I answered, "nobody can be knee-deep in this world without being able to recognize our own." It was a barb meant for Harvey as well, but he didn't take any notice of it.

"Jack is a special case," the sergeant answered, "and not up for discussion."

The standard government response wasn't unexpected, but I wasn't about to let it slide. "In the spirit of cooperation, you know me and what I can do. I would appreciate it if you saved me the effort of finding out for myself."

Harvey's shoulders sagged, and he let out a sigh. "A few years ago, the United States caught wind of the German's attempts to create the ultimate warrior. They got their hands on a formula that allowed them to reanimate the dead in various states of viability. From your record, I'm guessing that you've ran into a few of them."

"You could say that," was the only answer I supplied. In truth, I had developed a habit of fighting various types of Nazi undead and was getting tired of it. "So, Jack is a corpse?"

"No," Harvey answered quickly. "We're not Germans and the dead aren't so easily controlled. We came at this with an American mindset. We wanted to make something better."

Jack uncovered his head to reveal a normal human face with close-cropped hair and a small amount of stubble. There was nothing weird about him at all.

Until I saw the sweat.

We were in the Namibian desert, driving across sand and patches of dried grass with the sun beating down on us. We were all sweating in the heat, but Jack was sweating profusely and his sweat had an oily texture to it.

I brought up my gun quicker than Nancy could stop me and cocked the hammer.

Everybody was shouting but the only voice I could make out was Nancy's.

"What are you doing?"

I didn't pull the trigger right away only because this thing was driving the vehicle we were in. I didn't much care for our would-be saviors, but I wasn't about to endanger Nancy unless I had to.

"He's a damned shoggoth," I hissed.

"No, he's not," Tim said. I noticed that his pistol was aimed at me.

"I've seen shoggoths before." I ignored Tim's gun and kept mine raised.

"Yes," Harvey explained, "he is a shoggoth, but not in the way you think."

Shoggoths were servants to the Old Ones. Shapeless forms of malleable flesh that fed on humanity both physically and through the consumption of their souls. When they weren't trying to blend in, they tended to be fifteen-foot-wide oily blobs of eyes, teeth, and tentacles. Over the centuries, humanity had tried over and over again to enslave the shoggoths, but we just didn't know the secret that the Old Ones did.

The sweat was what gave Jack away. Shoggoths don't operate well during daylight. It's harder for them to keep their forms together.

They were monsters and they needed to die.

"Explain faster." I tightened my grip on my pistol.

"He's a hybrid, and the only successful one we made before we scrapped the program." Harvey twisted in his seat to look at me and my pistol. "The government needed something better than the German's dead soldiers and they knew they couldn't control a shoggoth. Somebody had the bright idea of making a shoggoth that thought it was human. Out of ten subjects, the only success was Jack."

Nancy frowned, "A shoggoth with a soul?"

Nancy had spent much of her last moments with her father fleeing from the ancient form of a proto-shoggoth. She knew what these creatures were capable of.

"Something like that," Harvey nodded. "We grafted a soldier's brain to the remains of a shoggoth's body. We revived both of them with the formula the Reich was using."

"What happened to the other nine?" I demanded.

Harvey didn't answer right away. After a moment, he said, "They went insane and killed themselves."

I nodded toward Jack, who continued to drive and watch the road ahead as if I didn't have a gun aimed at him. "What made him special?"

"We think a combination of things," Tim put his pistol away under an assumption that I wasn't really going to shoot our driver. "He was the youngest test subject, he was recently deceased, he had family, and he was part of the USEC before he died."

The last part convinced me, at least in part, to lower my gun. I didn't lower the hammer, though. "He knew what he signed up for. He was the only person you used who wasn't surprised by the outcome."

Harvey nodded. "Since then, he's been quieter than when he was alive, but he follows orders and he gets the job done."

I turned to Nancy, "That's the problem with people. They're always making the same mistakes. Every shoggoth that humans have tried to enslave has followed orders until it wasn't convenient for them anymore. Then they killed everyone."

"Dr. Doran," Jack said, startling both Nancy and me. His voice sounded normal for a human in his mid-twenties. "I don't know what I am, and I don't expect you to trust me, but I am certainly not your problem. I want to help people and have no interest in killing anyone. Besides," he smiled and I found it entirely unnerving, "the USEC has better weapons than your magic peashooter."

I released the hammer on my pistol and slid it back into my satchel. "If it's alright with you, we're going to keep our distance for now."

Jack nodded and didn't say another word for the rest of the drive.

After about an hour of driving, Jack parked the jeep near a series of small tents and quickly erected buildings on the western coast of Namibia. Neither Nancy or I took our eyes off of our driver for the entire ride. Shoggoths everywhere knew me and wanted me dead. I wasn't about to let one that was within an arm's length have the jump on me.

When the vehicle stopped, Harvey and Tim led us into a small building. The debriefing lasted hours, but that had more to do with giving the United States Esoteric Calvary time to look over the Book of Eibon than it did with getting any sort of valuable knowledge from us.

Finally, they put Nancy and me into the same room and left us alone. I figured they could hear us, but I didn't care what they knew.

"How'd it go?" I asked my assistant.

Nancy shrugged before taking a seat across the table from me, where the interrogators had previously sat. "They mostly asked questions about you and my father. You?"

"They asked me everything that I might know about the Book of Eibon. I told them we should probably start calling it a scroll."

She crossed her arms. "What happened back there? I thought the Traum Kult were gone?"

"Your guess is as good as mine," I explained. "Anita gathered the remains and is trying to reform it under her own agenda."

"And what would that be?" Nancy asked.

I shrugged. "Whatever it is, it won't be good. The Traum Kult have spent the last three hundred years working for the highest bidder and ... something else. They are psychics and wizards who want a closer connection to their gods. To do that, they'll bring Hell to Earth." I let out a sigh. "At least when they were controlled by the Nazis, we could guess what they wanted."

Raising an eyebrow, I changed the subject. "Now that we know a little more about my sword, do you want to share what you know about my pistol?"

Nancy smiled. "I was wondering when you were going to get around to asking me again."

"I've been distracted," I answered, but it was an understatement. When we had left Antarctica, all I knew was that the German army was trying to get another powerful book and there had been no time to talk about how my gun was made. Between then and now, this was the first time that we had both had a chance to sit and talk about anything unrelated to her father's journal.

"Your pistol belonged to Eliot Ness," Nancy explained.

"The Chicago cop who put away Capone?" I asked, incredulous.

Nancy gave a slight nod. "I was studying in Chicago when I started the hunt for my father and one of the first things I came across was a magical gun that had disappeared after Eliot Ness visited Arkham. According to a retired policeman I interviewed, Capone wasn't just moving booze; he'd also hired the kind of people we run into. Ness needed something to fight back." She shrugged. "I don't know where he got the gun, but he called it the Equalizer, because it evened the odds for him and the rest of his men."

I leaned back in my chair and folded my arms, impressed. "Is that true?"

"As far as I know," Nancy answered. "If we ever find out where the pistol was made, I'll need to get myself one."

"That'll be a cold day in Hell." The smile dropped from my face.

"What?" Her brow furrowed with confusion as she leaned back. "I can't have a pistol as useful as yours?"

"No, you can't," I answered, "but Nancy can."

"What?" She asked again.

"I've been hunting monsters for a very long time." I scooted my chair away from the table and stood up, preparing for whatever might happen next. "I smelled the void on you the minute you walked in here, Jack."

When I said the hybrid's name, Nancy's flesh shifted and then reformed into that of the USEC driver.

I waved my hand at him, "Did you make the stuff about my gun up or were you reading her mind?"

He shook his head. "Neither. That's the story she told us during her debriefing." He held up his hand to silence me. "Before you get upset, this wasn't a test for you. They sent me in here as part of my training, to see how I could blend in against someone of your skills." He stood from his chair and let out a sigh. "Obviously, I failed."

Uncharacteristically of me, I felt sympathy for the monster. Before he left, I said, "A word of advice?"

He stopped and looked at me, and I couldn't get over how human the thing looked. "Yes?"

"An enemy with my skills isn't someone you hide from," I said, "it's someone you kill." It was chillingly honest, and I couldn't help but think of the psychic assassins in the Traum Kult. I was a novice compared to most of them. If Jack was truly on the side of right, he wouldn't survive trying to convince one of the cultists that he was human.

Jack nodded and left the makeshift interrogation room without saying anything else.

The real Nancy Dyer joined me a few minutes after Jack left. The way she explained it, Jack had pulled the same stunt on her, but disguised as me.

"He blew his cover when he asked me about my father's death," she explained. "You were there, and you know better than to bring it up."

Sergeant Harvey Neil came into the room only seconds later with a large bag slung over his shoulder. "We're done with both of you and have a plane standing by to take you and the Book of Eibon back to the States."

"That's it?" Nancy asked. "You save us from two armies, interrogate us, and then let us go? That doesn't add up."

Harvey nodded. "You're right, that's not everything." He unslung the bag and set it on the table. Unzipping it revealed all of our items and a black rubber tube about a foot long.

I picked up the tube and inspected it before pulling off the cap. Inside was the original Hyperborean book: The Scroll of Eibon.

"Also," Harvey said, "the USEC thinks it would be wise if one of our groups took up residence in Arkham. Perhaps within a mile of the university."

"You're not bringing a shoggoth to my city," I blurted out.

"Back down, Doctor," Harvey barked. "If you've got a problem with Jack, then fight him already. Otherwise, shut your hole and listen up." He pointed to the rubber cylinder. "The Traum Kult and the Germans are after that, and that doesn't include the crazies who live in your town. While you might be able to handle a pistol, the USEC isn't willing to trust Miskatonic University on their ability to keep an all-powerful book out of enemy hands." He let out a long sigh. "Even you can't be everywhere, Doran."

It pained me to admit it, but Sergeant Neil had a point. Getting the Scroll of Eibon was only half the battle. We still need to ensure that it would remain in our hands. If I were to get swept up into another artifact hunt, it wouldn't be fair to leave my secretary, Carol Berg, guarding the powerful tome. She was formidable, but no match for psychics and whatever the Germans could throw at us.

"Who will be joining us, then?" I asked.

"Myself, Private Ruddel, and Jack," Harvey answered aggressively, expecting me to again protest Jack's joining us.

While that had been my knee-jerk reaction, I couldn't deny the benefits of having the hybrid along. If Jack was everything that he said he was, he would be an invaluable asset in any fight.

If he wasn't, then there was nobody better at killing shoggoths than I was.

"Fine, but I'm to be made aware anytime that you want on campus." That would give me at least some idea of Jack's location at most times. "And you're not allowed inside the armory."

"We do not report to you, civilian." Harvey couldn't mask the annoyance in his voice.

I didn't flinch from his tone. "No, but you're going to need my cooperation and the only way you get that is if I know where you are when you're on my campus."

"You'll be storing the scroll there, then? At the armory?" Harvey said, never agreeing to let me know where he was.

Nodding, I answered, "We both know that it's the safest place in Arkham for it. If you need to get in there, it'll be with me accompanying you."

He didn't like it, but Harvey agreed. "Your plane is waiting. The sooner we put Namibia behind us, the more distance we can put between ourselves and our enemies."

We made our way to the plane. It was a seaplane, parked near at least four more identical to it and without many markings. There was a single star in a circle with a line running behind it— the symbol regularly used to mark American military aircraft. I didn't know planes at all, but it was large enough for the group of us but not much more. The sergeant said that we would be making a few stops along the way for refueling. While I didn't enjoy the idea of being cooped up with a shoggoth thing and the military's answer to the Traum Kult, it would be much faster than the boat that Nancy and I had booked. With the Atlantic plagued with German U-boats, it would be much safer, too.

The Armory

The cramped military plane stopped only once between the coastal Namibian base and Arkham, Massachusetts. Along the way, Sergeant Neil told us a little about our taxi. The plane was called a Martin PBM Mariner, a type of long-range bomber being implemented by the United States military for reconnaissance and bombing missions. Our first stop was in Belém, Brazil. We landed directly in the Gualá River, and there were hundreds of other planes already there. Harvey said the planes were on rotation and constantly on the search for German subs.

Belém was home to a combined Army Air Corps and Navy base surrounded by the thick jungle. We stayed in the plane as a tractor came down a wide ramp. Soldiers hooked the front of our plane to the tractor and pulled us out of the water to refuel. Nancy and I stayed the night near the edge of the Amazon. We had dinner with the United States Esoteric Cavalry. It was only the two men and Jack. I still wasn't sure how to label him. The rest of the soldiers on the base didn't have any idea what the USEC were, but they knew they weren't supposed to ask and mostly avoided them and us. We woke up a little before six in the morning to planes taking off. That was our signal to pack our bags and load into the plane. The sun was climbing above the trees and while it was beautiful, I looked forward to getting home.

We left Belém and flew the rest of the distance to Massachusetts, landing in the Miskatonic River that my university was named after. There were no tractors or ramps with army personnel waiting for the PBM as we landed. Instead, we motored to the nearest pier and unloaded from there. The pilot returned to the skies after we had unloaded all of our and the USEC's gear.

Nancy and I made our way to a nearby house with a dock, parting ways with our USEC team without ceremony. We knew we would see each other again soon, and neither group was looking forward to it. The house belonged to a pleasant older couple. They loaned us their phone and Nancy called the admissions office at Miskatonic University. They offered to send a car for us. We thanked the couple for letting us use their phone and waited outside and closer to the road so that the car would see us. Within the hour we were back in my office at the university.

Carol Berg, the administrative assistant assigned to my office and my nag of an office wife, was waiting for us at my desk. As Nancy and I walked in, Carol's head shot up from what she was reading, and she sniffed the air.

When not in her native form, Carol was a brunette with streaks of silver in her hair. She looked to be only a few years older than I was, but that wasn't true at all. Carol's wendigo nature made her practically immortal and her age was measured in centuries.

"You found it," she stated flatly. Her eyes had taken on a distant quality. Since we hadn't told her about our success during the brief arrangement for the car to pick us up, she must have sensed something of Hyperborea on the scroll or us.

Nancy held up the rubber tube like a trophy. "With surprisingly less resistance than we anticipated."

With more speed and grace than either Nancy or I could accomplish, Carol ran at us from behind the desk and grabbed the tube. As if her actions hadn't been her own, her face turned red with embarrassment and she slowly handed the tube back to Nancy.

"Sorry," she ran her hands down the front of her clothes and took a step back. "I don't know what came over me."

"Hyperborea gives you your strength," I explained. "This has been in that cave for centuries. It's imbued with the source of your natural power."

Carol snorted, but it was obvious that she found it difficult to take her attention off the scroll. "You mean curse, not strength."

I nodded, understanding her point.

"I suggest," Carol said slowly and with deep breaths, "that you take that directly to the armory."

The look in my secretary's eyes wasn't unknown to me. Normally, her eyes had that look when she was completely changed. I had never seen her with that ravenous hunger while still in her human form. She was barely keeping it together.

"That's a great idea." I told Carol before turning to Nancy, "You head that way, and I'm going to catch up on what I've missed since we left."

Nancy nodded without taking her attention from the predator in the room. Gathering her things, she backed out the door. When she could no longer see Carol, she turned and headed in the direction of the armory.

Once Nancy was out of earshot, I turned to Carol and touched her shoulder. She started at the touch. "Are you going to be alright?"

Carol nodded. "I should be. It had a … scent. I've never smelled anything like that before."

"Have you ever been to Hyperborea?" I asked as I walked her to an armchair.

She shook her head as she sat. "No, I was turned a long time ago, but that was in Canada," she rolled her eyes, "on Earth." Carol rubbed her face. "I'll be fine. You should go help your assistant before she fumbles herself into a weapon of untold horror in the armory."

"You sure?" I wasn't certain that Carol was feeling any better. Her skin had turned the pale white of her wendigo form. She still looked human, though.

Her head bobbed up and down in her hands. "I'm fine. I just need a moment to compose myself."

Trusting her, I made my way to the armory with all of my gear still on me.

My first trip to the armory had been shortly after the Traum Kult had stolen Miskatonic University's copy of the Necronomicon. To find my way, I had been given a magical coin that grew warmer the closer I got to the armory. It was simple coin magic and I had kept the coin, but hadn't had a reason to use it since.

I walked into the armory and began searching about for Nancy. There was only one of our display cases that I thought up to the task of holding this special document, and I doubted that Nancy knew which one it was.

Miskatonic's armory was less a weapon cache and more a museum of the rarest types of antiquities. Each item in the armory had, at some point in history, been imbued with esoteric and magical properties. No matter how mundane the artifact, if it was in the armory then it was too dangerous to be out in the world. This was where the world's secret history was kept.

Nancy was reading the provenience tag on an especially gruesome painting by a Bostonian artist named Richard Upton Pickman. It said a lot about the horrors that Nancy had already seen that she was able to examine the painting so closely without revulsion. Pickman was only considered a man by the very clinical definition. As far as I was concerned, he had thrown away his humanity the day he picked up a paint brush.

As I approached Nancy, I tried to keep my eyes away from the painting and instead focused on my assistant and the rubber tube in her hand.

"Try not to stare at it too long." I nodded toward the picture, still keeping my eyes from looking directly at it. "We don't need you any more traumatized than working with me has already made you."

Nancy pulled her eyes from the painting and I realized that her attention had never been on Pickman's portrait at all. Her thoughts were somewhere else entirely.

Before I could ask her about it, she held up the tube. "Where are we putting this?"

I nodded past her and down the aisle of artifacts toward the far wall of the armory. "Back there, come on." I started in that direction before she could argue with me. Once I knew that Nancy was in step behind me, I turned a bit and asked, "What's going on? You seem distracted."

Nancy sighed and out of the corner of my eye I saw her

shoulders sag. "A lot, actually." She paused before adding, "I think I need to leave."

I stopped and turned to face her, only a few yards from the glass case in which I wanted to place the Scroll of Eibon.

"Leave? I thought you were going to take Leo's place here at the university?"

Nancy shrugged. "I wanted to," she stopped and corrected, "I want to, but I don't know that I should. I came here to find my dad and I did. Since then, we haven't had a chance to stop and look around at the world that I'm now a part of." She lifted her tommy gun. "In what world does an assistant at a university carry a machine gun?"

I nodded. "This work isn't easy. We're not educating young minds, but protecting them from the real world. If you're not up for it, there's no shame in admitting that."

Nancy shook her head, "It's not that I'm not up for it." She let out another sigh. "It's all of that and—" she swung her finger back and forth between us, "and this. I've lost people that I care about and I don't know that I'll be able to handle losing us, too."

Us? My mind spun as I tried to figure out what she was saying until I realized that she was admitting something that, while I had felt it in the back of my mind, I hadn't had a chance to examine it.

"Us? You mean as a couple?" The way I said it sounded surprised, but I shouldn't have sounded that way. It made sense. She was very attractive, and we had worked together closely.

My surprise spread to Nancy's face. "Oh no. You weren't … I mean, I thought you were interested in …"

She cut off mid-sentence as her face turned red.

"Don't be embarrassed," I tried to recover. "It crossed my mind, but with everything going on and the things we had been through I hadn't had time to think on it." It was my turn to sigh. "I'm not the best at relationships. My last relationship was with a magical projection of my subconscious." I held up the tube containing the scroll. "Don't leave, yet. The USEC is in town and I'm going to need someone with me to stop me from killing the hybrid. It'll give us a little more time to see about … us. Then if you think leaving is the best idea, I won't stop you."

Nancy looked at me for a long moment and I felt like I was flirting back in school. In my world of monsters and alien feelings, this seemed the most alien to me, but I liked it.

Finally, Nancy gave me a small grin and nodded. In that moment, she looked less like my gun-toting assistant and more like the attractive young woman she was.

"That sounds like a plan, boss. Let's put that tube away."

I nodded and then heard a sharp whisper in my left ear.

"You should have let her go."

I spun, but no one was there. I turned back to Nancy.

"Did you hear that?"

She frowned, but tightened her grip on her gun. "Hear what?"

I did my best to dismiss it, at least outwardly. I didn't want to have to explain to Nancy that the voice, with its French accent, sounded eerily familiar.

Shaking my head, I replied, "Nothing, just tired from the flight still." Nancy lowered her gun but her grip didn't loosen.

In a vain effort to convince myself that it was all in my head, I pushed the strange voice from my head and turned back to the glass case.

Previously, the glass case had held the Al-Azif, the first draft and living version of the Necronomicon, as written by the mad Abdul Alhazred. The glass was covered in protective warding as well as insect nests and webbing. It was almost too difficult to see through it all, but it would make the perfect place to keep the scroll for now.

The warding that stopped anyone from opening the case except for the Dean of Miskatonic University had been down since I removed the Al-Azif. If the Al-Azif had survived my adventure to northern New York, I would have replaced the book here and turned the warding and locks back on. Since that wasn't the case, I was safe to open the glass and did so, lifting it up and sliding it back into the shelving.

I decided to leave the scroll in the rubber tubing, as it wouldn't hurt to have that extra bit of protection on it and I didn't want to handle the scroll with my bare hands any more than I had to.

"Give it to me!" a voice hissed from the entrance to the armory.

Nancy and I spun and saw a monster running on all fours toward us. It took me a moment longer than it should have to recognize Carol in her wendigo form as she rushed at us. My first thought was to grab at my pistol, but I stopped myself and stepped forward, using the tube to lower Nancy's tommy gun.

"Don't shoot her, she's not in her right mind," I explained.

"If she tries to kill me, she's getting a bullet." Nancy wasn't being unreasonable. She was a survivor, and that was one of the things that I found both useful and interesting about her. Being a survivor meant everything in our line of work.

I almost handed off the tube with the scroll to Nancy before it occurred to me that Carol was headed straight for it. I put the leather strap attached to the tube over my shoulder and slid the scroll behind my back.

"Keep your gun ready." I pulled my own pistol from its holster and handed it to Nancy. "I don't want her killing me either." Bringing up my index finger, I risked turning back to Nancy quickly and added, "Only as a last resort."

"I can help." Nancy said it only half-heartedly, not certain how she could help me fight a fully enraged wendigo while surrounded by supernatural landmines.

"You are helping," I countered.

The best thing that I could do would be to put the scroll into the glass case and turn the wardings back on. Unfortunately, Carol wasn't going to give me enough time to do any of that and Nancy didn't know how.

"Carol," I called out to my charging secretary. "You don't want to do this. It's not you, it's the scroll. It's Hyperborea calling out to you. You're stronger than this."

Carol was a magnificent example of a wendigo. Her features were elongated, with her fingers ending in black talons. Her eyes had sunk into her head and the sockets were dark. Her flesh was as pale as death and while she still wore her dress, she had found the wherewithal to take off her shoes before the transformation had destroyed them. Even her hair had transitioned into a straw-like and wispy approximation of what it had been.

Carol's transformation had turned her more into an animal than a person, and her mouth was where the beast was most visible. Her face had stretched several inches to make room for the changes inside of her mouth. Her teeth were almost as long as her new talons and were sharp enough that her lips were already bleeding from shouting at us.

Something in what I said resonated with the beast and she slowed. She shook her head as my words reached past the wendigo and touched Carol's mind.

It didn't last long. Whatever was calling to her from Hyperborea was stronger than Carol was. One final shake of her head and the wendigo resumed rushing at me.

Instinctively, I reached out to the void to create a shield between us. Before I could create the shield, the void overwhelmed me with the different energies being radiated by the armory's artifacts. There was a raging storm of energy throughout the room and me using a spell would be like grabbing a lightning bolt from the sky. Even if I could pull it off, I had no idea the effects to me if I succeeded.

Before I closed myself off to the void, I saw a part of the storm radiating from behind me and shining brighter than almost everything else in the armory. I didn't have to check the tube to know that it was the magic of Hyperborea and the thing that was calling to my secretary.

Without using magic, I didn't know how I was going to stop an enraged wendigo, but I had to try. I didn't know why the scroll wanted Carol to have it, but letting the monster get the magical totem was generally a bad idea.

"Get down," I shouted behind me and hoped that Nancy reacted quickly enough. I dove to the left as Carol reached me, slamming my body into a shelf of books and miscellaneous rocks. The shelf rocked and spilled some of its contents, but I didn't slow. Diving forward, I slid under a nearby table and into the next aisle of curated artifacts.

I came up beside an antlered deer head, lying back on its mounted board. Its eyes held a certain malice as they looked between me and Carol.

Carol corrected her trajectory, missing Nancy entirely, and

dove through the table that I had slid under. As she came up to me, I scooped up the possessed bit of taxidermy and swung it at Carol. Only barely getting the head up in time, I was lucky enough to catch Carol across the side of her face.

Not phased at all, she lunged at me again. I twisted the head and brought the antlers up to deflect her swing. Instead of deflecting her attack, the antler pierced Carol's arm. She howled in pain and I could see her rage turn to hunger at the scent of the blood.

Wendigo weren't just transformative monsters unlucky enough to be given a curse. The wendigo curse was an unfortunate side effect of cannibalism. At some point in Carol's supernaturally long life, she had been down on her luck enough that eating human flesh had been her only means of survival. The effect had meant her survival, but only as the transformed beast that was now attacking me.

When a wendigo's eyes fill with hunger, it means that they want to eat you.

Carol didn't pull the antler out of her arm. Instead, she yanked her arm away, tearing the taxidermized head from my hands and letting its momentum pull it from her arm. Blood trailed behind her as she stalked toward me, and I knew that wound would heal soon.

It'd heal even quicker if she managed to tear into my throat.

Wendigo were faster and stronger than normal people. It was believed that in eating the flesh of another person, they gained that person's power. So, it came to reason that a wendigo that was a few centuries old, even a domesticated one that hadn't hunted people for at least a century, would be many times stronger than the average person.

Without the void to defend myself with, I was left with few options. I turned and sprinted toward the entrance to the armory. She was much faster than I was, so I leaped over tables and knocked over shelves as she rushed at me and the scroll.

My eyes darted across the shelves and tables as I ran, looking for anything that I could use to stop her. I saw an enchanted two-hundred-year-old Faro deck that wouldn't do me any good, as I didn't think Carol was in the mood for a card game. The next table had a large stuffed doll made of bright green fabric. I wasn't entirely sure what I was looking at for a moment, but then I realized that it was a caricature of Cthulhu made in a style that I could only assume was meant to be cute. Sitting beside the doll that must have been intended for converting children was a mammoth tusk with Inuit scrimshaw covering it. I didn't need to read the provenience card tied to it, as I had been the one who wrote it. There was a map hidden in the scrimshaw, designed to lead the user somewhere. I hadn't figured out the where, yet.

Then my eyes landed on something that could be useful. When I wasn't using my time as a student at Miskatonic to study the occult and its misuse throughout the world, I had taken a shining to the Mesoamerican cultures. Specifically, that of the Aztecs.

The Aztecs had been a people that believed in sacrifice. They would pull out the hearts of their captured enemies and hope that the blood would be enough to appease the gods.

On the table I was running directly toward was a large obsidian blade. The Blade of the Winged-Serpent, Quetzalcoatl.

I grabbed it and swung wide at Carol, trying to scare her off of me more than anything. She stopped short and eyed me, but the look on her face showed me that she wasn't entirely lost to the beast. Carol had a better knowledge of the armory than I ever would. She had been there when it was first formed and had spent much of her unnatural life cataloging it. When she saw that I held the Blade of the Winged-Serpent, her beastly visage smirked.

I took a second swipe at my secretary before I was hit by the blade's power. The souls of every person that it had ever killed started screaming in my mind. Distantly, I remembered that the blade was meant to capture the pain of each of its victims. It was meant to ensure that the blade wouldn't be used except in the most dire of circumstances.

While my situation fit that description, I didn't have the strength for all of that pain and dropped the blade.

Obsidian is incredibly fragile, but this was no ordinary blade. Instead of shattering when it hit the ground, it landed roughly and slid under the nearest bookshelf.

My head was still spinning, and I clutched at my chest as the ghost of so many hearts being ripped from it continued to haunt me.

When I finally opened my eyes and realized that I should be dead, I looked around for where my would-be assassin might have disappeared to.

I didn't have to look far to find Carol vaulting over shelves toward where Nancy ran for the armory door. I grabbed at the nearest books that didn't seem to be possessed and threw them as hard and fast as I could. On the third attempt, one of them struck the wendigo in the back of the head. She spun, looking over her shoulder for her newest attacker. Seeing just me with literary projectiles annoyed her, but she'd already come to realize that Nancy was the one holding the scroll.

What she didn't realize is that I didn't need to vault over tables to cross the aisles of artifacts. As slight as the distraction had been, Carol's hesitation had given me enough time to close the distance by sliding and rolling under the few tables between us.

Carol was returning her attention to Nancy as I came up behind her. Nancy was still too far from the door. If I didn't stop Carol, she would tear my assistant apart to get to that damned scroll.

I leaped onto Carol's back and could feel her muscles flex as she reached over her head with her clawed hands to grab me. I dropped before she grabbed me, ducking as she spun with incredible speed to swipe at my abdomen. She missed, only barely, before kicking out and striking me in the chest. I slammed back into two shelves of artifacts. They cascaded down around me, and I barely managed to avoid getting my head crushed by an empty Mi-Go brain jar. When they weren't falling off of shelves, these were normally used for the safe transfer of human brains across the universe to be used in whatever sick plans the Mi-Go had. My interest was pulled from the high-tech jar to the artifacts that it landed beside, and I suddenly had an idea for stopping Carol.

For part one of my stupid plan, I scooped up a boomerang covered in Yithian script and threw it with surprising accuracy at Carol's back. More surprisingly, Carol twisted and grabbed the spinning hunk of wood without even looking at it. More importantly, though, she again stopped her advance toward Nancy, buying the woman more time as she inched closer to the door.

Her hesitation was all I needed to flip the switch on the device whose card read "Tillinghast Resonator." The machine was as long as the shelf it rested on and looked to be made from parts of an old radio. What I remembered of Tillinghast and his research was sparse at best, but his research focused on allowing those without the touch of magic to peek beyond the veil between worlds.

The second that I flipped the switch the air was filled with floating insect-like things. Worms and grubs and creatures entirely too alien to describe floated in the air, migrating through the shelves and walls of the armory as if they weren't there. In a way, they weren't. This device seemed to do what I did naturally every time that I reached out for the touch of magic. It made the alien worlds from beyond the veil, sharing the same space as ours but not the same frequency, visible for normal people.

And wendigo.

Carol ducked the first two creatures as they swarmed toward her. She tried to grab the next one, but her hands went right through. Her monster form wasn't realizing that these creatures weren't in our world, and therefore she couldn't grab them. My secretary let out a roar that triggered a state of instinctual fear deep inside me.

Ignoring the floating monstrosities, I closed the distance to Carol and pressed the wooden dagger into her pale bicep. The card, still tied to the handle and dangling beneath my hand, read "Svefnthorn".

While I consider myself well-versed in the cultural narratives of most of the world, I'll be the first to admit that my Norse Mythology is rusty. That's why seeing the bright red underline on the provenience card had caught my attention more than the odd name of the dagger. The word that was underlined was "Sleep." The Svefnthorn was also known as the "Sleep Thorn" and had been used to knock out the Norse Gods for whatever pranks they were in the mood for.

Carol looked down at the dagger as I pulled it from her arm before collapsing to the floor. She was unconscious.

The Office

After Nancy and I had secured the scroll in the glass case, we each grabbed an end of Carol and carried her up to my office. We secured her to my desk chair with the strongest ropes we could find in the maintenance closet. If this were any other school, I would wonder why my school had so much rope. Unfortunately, Carol wasn't the first monster that we've had to secure, and she was more than likely not going to be the last.

Once Carol was secured to the chair, Nancy turned to me and sighed.

"What the hell just happened?"

I shrugged. "Which part?" I looked at the stack of mail that had collected while Nancy and I were chasing the scroll across the world. The top letter was from London, England and the Special Operations Executive. I didn't know much about that branch, but from what I did know they were the English equivalent of the USEC. I had more pressing things on my mind and pushed the letter to the back of my mind.

"All of it." Nancy pointed at Carol's still unconscious form. "Why is a monster working here if she can't control herself, for starters?"

"Carol is in complete control," I explained. "I think that whatever just happened was related to the Scroll of Eibon?"

"How is that possible?" Nancy sat on the edge of my desk and crossed her arms.

I pinched the bridge of my nose as I tried to compile the entire explanation in my head. "Eibon was a wizard of Hyperborea, and that scroll is infused with some of his power and some of the power of that land. Carol is a wendigo and wendigo get their power from an ancient connection with Hyperborea. I think that bringing the scroll into our world and in proximity to Carol pushed her back toward the monster she once was."

Nancy shook her head. "I've seen her change before; she still is that monster."

I shook my head. "I don't mean that it forced her to turn into a wendigo, I mean that the scroll removed her self-control." I sat next to the bookshelf and poured myself a small glass of the brandy that Leo kept on the shelf. "It made her the creature that she was a century ago."

"How does a monster like what we just saw," asked Nancy, "become the secretary to the Dean of Miskatonic University?"

The brandy's burn barely registered as I thought back to the first time that I had asked that same question. I was given a much less detailed answer than I was going to give Nancy, but Carol had given me the rest when she had learned that I could be trusted.

Before I could explain, I noticed blood dripping from Nancy's arm and onto the floor of my office. "You're bleeding."

Nancy looked down at her arm and twisted it to get a better view. A four-inch gash ran along her bicep. "Oh no..." Nancy's voice was weak.

I retrieved the first aid kit from my desk. It consisted of the usual tools and bandages as well as a small flask of more bourbon. The bourbon wasn't there for implied medical reasons, but instead to hide it from Leo and his insatiable tastes. I immediately set to cleaning and dressing her wound.

"Am I going to turn into a wendigo, now?" Nancy's voice was laced with fear and I couldn't help but feel sorry for her.

Shaking my head, I answered, "No, that's werewolves, and while they might be real, I've never seen one. Wendigo are entirely different."

Carol let out a sigh in her sleep and we both spared her a glance. "Carol isn't your normal wendigo. She's been here at Miskatonic in some capacity for longer than I or almost anyone else has been alive. Long before that, she was a member of a group of Canadian fur traders from way up north. Together with their families, her group would spend most of their time setting traps in different forests and moving from forest to town and then to forest again, circling as they collected their furs and sold them. It was a good life until a very bad winter." I tied the bandage off and noticed Nancy wince. I grabbed the flask from the kit, sipped it and gave the rest to her. She didn't wince as the bourbon hit her throat.

"One winter, almost two hundred years ago, twelve of them went into the woods to collect their traps and ended up trapped themselves. A blizzard hit and they couldn't find their way back out. Hypothermia claimed them first and then the starvation hit." I returned to my chair and took a seat. "In certain lands, when the wind blows cold enough, the magic of Hyperborea bleeds into our world. It's at those times that horrible acts can change a person." My finger pointed at Carol's still unconscious form. "They took to eating each other to stay alive. As Carol ate, she realized that she was getting stronger by absorbing the strength and power of each person she consumed. It wasn't just cannibalism of the flesh; it was cannibalism of the spirit. As she grew stronger and ate the last of her friends and family, Carol became addicted to that taste and power. She was uncontrollable and became feral. Her transition into a fully-developed wendigo was complete."

"Like she was in the armory," Nancy said.

I shook my head. "You haven't seen a fully out of control wendigo, and I hope that you never do. She spent years roaming those woods and killing anything she could find. First it was the rest of her group trying to find her, then it was hunters and travelers. She killed and consumed them all. Carol Berg was the most ferocious of her kind and completely unstoppable. For thirty years she owned those woods until her legend had grown enough that a group of hunters from a nearby village took it upon themselves to put her down. Carol killed all but one of the men, a traveler from Arkham, who saw her for what she really was."

"A human," Nancy provided.

"A victim," I offered. "Carol didn't ask to be what she was. It's the human condition to survive at all costs, and the magic of Hyperborea took advantage of her drive to live."

Nancy raised her eyebrow, "Why didn't she kill the man from Arkham?"

I shrugged. "When Carol told me this story, she said she didn't know, but I think it was his compassion. He spoke to her as a person, and not as a monster. For the first time since she had transformed into a wendigo thirty years before, Carol pushed the monster back down and wrestled her sanity back. His name was Daniel Morgan. He offered to help her learn to control her urges and Carol had nothing left to lose. They came all the way back here. He got her a job here at the university and she fell in love. She found that the more she felt human, the more control she had. She buried herself in her work and buried herself in him."

"What happened to him?" Nancy asked, but she already knew the answer.

"Old age claimed him, and it didn't matter how human she felt or how much he had loved her; Carol's wendigo nature means that she is essentially ageless." I sighed. "Surprisingly, she still manages to keep control over her monster. As far as I know, she's the world's only ever reformed wendigo."

"Until today." My assistant sipped her flask before she said it.

"No, today wasn't her. That scroll brought back more of the Hyperborean magic that originally transformed her. It was catnip for an addicted cat." I frowned and stared at Carol's prone form. "I'm surprised that it hit her as hard as it did, though. I didn't expect it to get worse than it was when we first arrived."

"What are we going to do about our other monster?" Nancy changed the subject, and it took me a moment to realize who she meant. I had almost forgotten about our government-owned shoggoth.

"Honestly, I was surprised that the United States Esoteric Cavalry still existed. I heard rumors that they were being absorbed into one of the other government-controlled supernatural defense groups." I shook my head. "Jack is essentially immortal, but there are ways to put down shoggoths if he gets out of control."

"I know." Nancy's look turned dark as she remembered

the last time I killed a shoggoth. "He's got to get out of control before we do anything, though. That means people are going to die."

She had a point, and I wasn't going to deny it. The only reason that I hadn't shot Jack on the spot was because his circumstance was entirely new to me. Maybe the government had found out how to control a shoggoth. "He might be on our side. I'm not going to trust him, but I'm not going to do something to anger the secret branch of the military."

"Why are the USEC here? If they wanted the scroll, they could have just taken it." Nancy wasn't wrong. I couldn't stop the government from repatriating anything from the armory, and they could have confiscated the scroll anywhere between Namibia and Arkham.

"The United States Government has always taken a special interest in Miskatonic University," I said by way of an answer. "Arkham and the school have been a place where the forces of darkness converge. I'm sure they've had a presence in Arkham for years, but what surprises me is that they've let us know they are here. We had to decipher your father's journal and put together the clues to discover the location of an ancient scroll that hasn't been found in centuries. The Traum Kult and the Germans showed up, which isn't too surprising. I'm sure the Germans have been watching me and my movements, and the Traum Kult probably got tipped off by some otherworldly source."

"But the USEC?" Nancy prodded.

My answer left me unsatisfied. "I don't know how they found us or the scroll, but it's obvious why they were there. They didn't want to take the scroll from us, but they definitely wanted to keep it out of the hands of America's enemies."

"Then why are they in Arkham?"

"I think they aren't done." I looked out the window. "Arkham has Nazis and Traum Kult spies hiding in her. The USEC brought a shoggoth into my city to protect the Scroll of Eibon."

Nancy's eyes went wide. "Germans are here?"

"You probably shouldn't be afraid of the Germans as much

as the Traum Kult, but yes and no. I don't think Germans are actually here, but I wouldn't doubt if they had cast some sort of charm on some of our students or something similar. Unfortunately, the Traum Kult is made up of magic users from more countries than just Germany and they can blend in just about anywhere. They'll be here and they could be anywhere."

"I think you're right," Nancy added. "They want to protect the scroll, but they also want it. They just know you'll put up a fight. They aren't going to take the scroll from you unless they have to, but they might try to convince you to hand it over."

Sergeant Harvey Neil wasn't about to let me keep anything quite as powerful as I assumed the Scroll of Eibon to be, but he wasn't an idiot, either. My reputation was well known among the USEC and he most likely knew that I wasn't going to give up anything in the armory without a fight.

As that thought crossed my mind, there was a sudden knock at the open door to my office. Nancy and I turned our heads to see Private Tim Ruddel standing there and staring at the unconscious form of my secretary.

I snapped my fingers to get his attention. "Is there a reason that you're here, Private?"

He nodded as his eyes swung to meet mine. "Yes. I need you to come with me. There's something that you have to see."

The Streets of Arkham

We followed the young soldier out of the building and into the streets directly in front of the campus. We were greeted by Jack standing in the center of the surprisingly empty streets. Not a single person could be seen, but vehicles were lining the roads and lights were still on in the shops and cafes. Everyone had cleared out.

Jack was carrying rifles and I was pleased to see he was keeping his promise to me. The monster-man hybrid wasn't standing on the campus grounds, but was instead on the far side of the street from the school.

Whether that was in some effort to keep honest with me or the result of the large number of protection wards throughout the campus, I didn't care.

He tossed Private Ruddel a rifle as we joined him in the middle of the street.

"Are you armed?" Jack asked Nancy and me.

"I'm suddenly wishing that we were," I answered.

Nancy was staring down the road trying to see what the USEC were facing toward, but it was either not here yet or too far down the street. "Should we be? What's going on?"

The private was the one who answered her while Jack looked over his weapon.

"We are not entirely sure," Ruddel explained. "The police band is reporting a mob of some sort moving toward the school. Person-on-person attacks of a nature that made the Sarge think that they were..." he paused as he tried to find the words, "not natural."

Jack joined the conversation and added, "Teeth. They are

biting and tearing at the flesh of everyone they come across. Reports are saying that normal bullets aren't working." He stepped closer to me and spoke in a much quieter voice. "Have you fought the dead before, Doctor?"

"You know that I have," I answered with complete certainty that the sergeant had a file with my life story and that he had shared it with the shoggoth, "but this is unheard of. This is Arkham, it's too obvious. Things here kill indiscriminately in the night. The void is weaker in the daylight. How is this happening?"

Nancy pointed at the gray sky. "What daylight? That might be part of it."

I nodded slowly, ignoring her sarcasm for the point that she was making. The overcast was darker than the forecast had implied when it called for sunshine all afternoon. Even the normally gloomy days in Arkham were never quite this dark. The sky was being affected by something supernatural.

"Where's Sergeant Neil?" I asked.

In response to my query, Jack turned and looked down the street. He raised his eyebrow only slightly as he noticed something that the rest of us couldn't sense.

"Incoming," was all that he said.

The private raised his rifle as we all turned to look where Jack was directing his attention. Jack raised his own rifle and his skin started to ripple in anticipation of whatever was coming.

Having no weapon didn't cause Nancy to pause as she stepped forward to see what was coming. I, on the other hand, reflexively reached out to the void in search of the magic I would need to protect us.

That was when the sergeant came sprinting around the corner of Main Street and toward us. He looked to be running as hard as he was capable of. Sergeant Neil was carrying his rifle in both hands and even as he closed the distance to us, I could make out dark red stains across his military clothing.

"Is he hurt?" Nancy asked.

Jack shook his head. "That isn't his blood."

Monsters came around the same corner the sergeant had just rounded.

"Are those..." Nancy hesitated as she tried to understand what she was seeing, "people?"

I shook my head and pulled more of the void to surround us, purposefully choosing not to surround Jack with my power. "Those are corpses." Private Ruddel and Jack opened fire on the coming horde. "Someone has animated the dead."

"A lot of them," Nancy added. She wasn't exaggerating. It looked like hundreds of dead people running after Sergeant Neil and he was leading them directly toward us.

"We have this," Neil shouted as he joined us and spun around. He brought his gun up and fired twice into the crowd before adding, "Go, get your weapons, and hurry back."

I almost asked how he expected to fight a city's worth of the dead when Jack showed me.

Slowly stepping toward the rushing monsters, Jack slung his rifle over his shoulder by the strap and threw out his arms. They transformed into amorphous tentacles that grew bones and teeth in random places. The newly formed tentacles extended to ridiculous lengths, but never lost their arm width. Jack's arms slammed into the first row of the dead, piercing them, devouring them, and tearing them apart. It was a terrifying and impressive display.

I had to grab Nancy by the arm to tear her eyes from the scene. Our eyes met in that instant and I knew that we were thinking the same thing: If we ended up having to fight Jack, it was going to be harder than the usual shoggoth.

Nancy led the rush back toward the administrative building. We needed our guns.

We were through the doors and running to my office when the first attackers who weren't dead came at us. It was two men, the same age as any of the students on campus and dressed in inconspicuous clothing. They tackled me from the side after Nancy ran by the first intersection in the hall. The combined pair drove me into the nearest wall. The impact against the old brick made me almost black out, but I stayed conscious as they took turns punching me.

One of them was suddenly off of me, and the slight reprieve from the attacks gave me a moment to open my eyes and properly block the remaining attacker. From the corner of my eye, I saw Nancy with her hand around the collar of my second attacker as she punched him in the throat and bounced his head off of the other side of the hall.

Bringing my forearms in and toward my torso, I blocked two more punches before landing a quick uppercut to his chin. He fell back and directly into Nancy's open arms as she grabbed him by the back of the collar and repeated the same move she'd used against the first.

"Thanks," I said to Nancy's back as she resumed sprinting toward my office.

Carol was still unconscious where we had left her. I checked to make sure she was still alright before heading to the bookshelf that I hid my weapons behind. Within minutes, Nancy and I were armed. I carried my .38 pistol and Cavalry sword while Nancy hefted her tommy gun. Both of us grabbed as much extra ammunition as we could. I filled my pockets with bullets while Nancy grabbed a satchel and filled it with extra rounds for her gun before slinging it over her shoulder.

Nancy gestured toward Carol. "Should we wake her up? We could use a raging and uncontrollable monster right now."

"Everyone thinks that until the monster is raging and uncontrollable at them." While I was referring to Carol, I couldn't help but think about Jack and when he might be raging and uncontrollable in our direction. I shook my head. "She's going to stay tied up until I can figure out how to weaken the Hyperborean influence."

"You're probably right," Nancy agreed. "I'd rather not have to worry about a wendigo while also fighting Arkham's recently-evacuated cemeteries." She paused before adding, "Or a shoggoth with a gun."

"Don't remind me," I mumbled as I headed toward the door.

"Will she be safe here?" Nancy asked.

"This is probably the safest place in Arkham, or at least in the university. I'll lock the door and put up wards as we leave." Smirking, I added, "Besides, I pity the idiots that try to storm in here with a wild wendigo."

We locked up the office and set the wards just in time for

three students to turn down the hallway and come at us. The two on the right were both men while the one on the left was a woman. The man in the middle was carrying a double-barreled shotgun that was aimed in my general direction. The other two were holding their hands up with their palms out. It didn't take any great deduction on my part to recognize an attack stance of a spellcaster. From there, it was no giant leap to realize that these "students" were actually Traum Kult plants. All three of them were dressed in the kind of generic clothing that could hide them among the local student populace. Hell, they might even have been enrolled as students and waiting patiently for an order to attack.

When each of the student occultists stopped only ten feet away, Nancy let out a long and dramatic sigh.

"I thought that you said the wards in this place would make guns useless?" She waved at the shotgun aimed at my midriff. "That doesn't look useless."

I almost missed her wink.

Nodding, I picked up my end of the charade. "They won't. If a gun is fired on campus the wards destroy the shooter."

The gunman's two companions spared quick glances at him and then his gun before side-stepping away from him. He took a moment to try and see the wards around the hall, pausing briefly as his eyes landed on the door to my office. It was obvious that he couldn't read those wards, or he would have known them as simple protection spells. Instead, the moment he saw them he turned his attention down and to his shotgun.

That's when I drew my pistol and shot him in the forehead.

In the same movement, I twisted and pushed down on Nancy's own gun as she was lifting it to finish off the remaining cultists.

"We need these two alive," I told her. As I said it, I could hear the hard edge in my voice, recognizing it as much colder than I intended. It was getting too easy to kill and keep working as if nothing had happened. Not for the first time in my career, it made me question how much of my humanity I was losing to my quest against the veil. It made me worry about any sort of relationship with Nancy. If she was falling for me, was she falling for the cold-blooded killer that I was becoming, or the archaeologist and teacher that I was?

That thought flashed through my mind as Nancy and I rushed the remaining two cultists. The man on the right side of the hall was short but made of layered muscles upon muscles. He was either someone who spent much of his time working on his physique or had gained supernatural aid in increasing his physical strength.

When I slammed into him it was like trying to knock over a wall. My arms went around his waist and I tried to drive him to the ground like I had seen our campus football team do on multiple occasions. Unfortunately, he had different plans and brought both of his fists down on the center of my back, driving me to the ground.

I glanced over to see Nancy leaping at the other cultist while the magic user waved her hands about in an attempt to call forth some offensive spell. A blast of energy hit Nancy and she began gasping for breath and clutching at her throat.

I rolled to the side as the brawler brought his foot down where my head had been, and raced to my feet. As I lunged toward my assistant in hopes of helping her, the brawler grabbed me by my collar and pulled me back. I slammed into the wall with enough force to see stars.

The benefit to being in that position was that I had been cornered like this before and while the Traum Kult's brawler might have me beat on strength, I had yet to see anything to indicate that he was capable of moving quickly.

The stars were still fading from my eyes when I saw his fist coming at my head. I slid to the left and heard the wall shudder as his fist collided with it and the weaker protection wards covering it. A square foot of plaster exploded from where his hand had connected.

While I continued to duck his blows, I was incapable of getting to Nancy's side. I watched helplessly from the corner of my eye as my assistant fell to her knees. She was suffocating and there was nothing that I could do about it.

The sorceress had become complacent and had sauntered closer to her victim. That was when Nancy leapt to her feet with renewed strength. She pushed the cultist into the wall. Surprise covered her face as Nancy drew back her fists and began punching her with all of her might.

After the third punch bounced the sorceress' head off of the wall, she slumped to the ground unconscious.

To my relief, Nancy let out a loud gasp, taking in as much air as her starving lungs would allow.

During all of this, I was still ducking the brawler's fists and letting them get bloodied as they slammed into the wall. Twice, a fist glanced off my arm or my head and I reeled from the pain, but I kept up my dance, avoiding every attack that he aimed in my direction. My plan was simple, I just needed to keep avoiding his punches and moving further down the hall.

Finally, we were where I needed to be to end this fight. The brawler surprised me with two fast hooks that almost took me out of the fight, but when he came in for the third punch it was on a direct trajectory. I moved out of the way of the punch only barely, but instead of staying on my feet as I had before, I dove to the floor and covered my head.

The brawler's fist slammed into my warded office door. Bright lights and a loud explosion filled the hallway.

"I thought you said not to kill them," Nancy shouted over the ringing in her ears.

Looking over my shoulder, I could see why she thought he was dead. The Traum Kult's brawler had been turned to stone by the spells covering my door. He was the consistency and rust-colored red of Potsdam Sandstone.

"He's not dead," I said. "The stone acts as an anchor to this reality so that we can move him somewhere convenient before bringing him back."

Nancy was still taking deep breaths. "Bring him back? Bring him back from where?"

I shrugged. "He's in some big empty space between the dimensions. It's emptier than anything you could possibly imagine and if he's there too long he might go insane from the complete lack of anything." I nodded toward the sorceress. "Good job figuring out that if you knocked her out the spell would end."

Her eyes went wide for a brief moment before Nancy composed herself and rubbed her neck. "Sure, that's what I figured out."

I tested the weight of the cultist-turned-statue as Nancy's words came together in my mind. Smirking, I asked, "You had no idea that would happen, did you?"

Nancy shook her head. "I just wanted her to die before I did."

The cultist weighed less than I assumed he would have weighed in flesh, which made moving him easier than it would have been otherwise. We tilted him and dragged the cultist into the office and over to the corner furthest from my desk. We put his surviving friend in the chair across from my desk and bound her to it. Nancy took position and trained her gun on the statue.

I pushed her gun down gently. "We don't have time to interrogate them." I pointed out the window. "I don't know if you've noticed, but the city is under siege."

She waved at the statue. "You just said that if he's in there too long, he'll go insane."

"He'll at least be alive, which is more than the people of our city will be able to say if we don't move now."

Nancy wasn't budging. "They are Traum Kult, aren't they? What if they're the people behind this? They might know how to stop it."

Damn her logic. She had a point that I had been willfully ignoring. I didn't like seeing the USEC fighting to save my college while I was stuck in my office. That didn't change the fact that cultists on my campus at this moment was too convenient. I still wanted to be in the streets with the USEC, but Nancy was right.

"Fine." I put my hand back onto the top of her gun. "This is going to have to be fast and you probably aren't going to like it."

A puzzled expression crossed her face. "What does that mean?"

"It means that I'm going to have to do something dangerous," I answered.

The statue turned back into a gibbering cultist as I touched his shoulder and spoke the return word. He clawed at his eyes as he shimmied into the corner, screaming. When he pulled his hands off of his eyes and saw me his madness seemed to fall away, and the former statue lunged at me.

Before he could touch me, I grabbed the sides of his head and began chanting. His eyes turned white as the pupils rolled back into his head. I had no idea what it looked like I was doing from Nancy's perspective, but she let out a gasp right before I entered the Traum Kult brawler's mind.

To the cultist, it looked as though we were walking through the halls of an alien cavern lined with scrolls. I didn't know if this was something from his memories or if it was a side-effect of the magic. This was the first time that I'd ever used this spell, so a lot of this was new to me.

"Why are you in my school?" I asked. He stood across from me, wearing nothing except tattoos of protective spells. Unfortunately for him, none of them were aimed at protecting him from me.

"We've been here for years," he answered without hesitation. "We have been watching you, watching Miskatonic, and waiting for orders."

"From the Traum Kult?"

He smirked. "Does that matter?"

I clenched my fist and a row of scrolls against the nearest wall burst into flame. The cultist began screaming and raised his hand up to his face. It was turning gray and the flesh was starting to decay. His hand fell off and vanished before it could hit the floor.

"What is happening?"

It was my turn to smirk. "We're inside your head and I'm burning your soul. Every lie you tell me, or any time that I think you're wasting my time, I will destroy another part of you and I won't stop until you are a hollow husk drooling on my office carpet."

"Fine!" He was shouting. "That's not what they call themselves anymore, but yes. I was waiting for orders from them."

"What are they called now?" I couldn't hide the surprise on my face.

Before he could answer, he screamed again, and the fire leapt from the first row of scrolls and to the next. His entire arm fell off. The damage I had caused was spreading and I was running out of time.

"Why did you attack me now?"

He was gritting his teeth. "We were told that you had the scroll and would be vulnerable if we moved now."

"How many of you are here?"

"I don't know." The decay started on his other hand. "I don't know!" He shouted louder. "They don't tell us until we get our orders."

I tried to halt the decay and burning to buy some more time. It seemed that my control over the spell was nonexistent.

"Did you send the dead to my school?" I stepped closer to him and he flinched.

"The what?" Both of his arms were gone and the decay had climbed each of his legs.

"The army of the dead crawling over the city to get to Miskatonic!" I was shouting, too.

He fell to his knees as his ankle bones turned to dust and the decay spread to his abdomen. "I don't know anything about that." His voice was a whimper now. "Please," he begged, "stop this."

It was horrifying and worse than I had anticipated. The rushed torture of this man hadn't only crossed my personal lines, but he was well beyond any sort of recovery. If I could end it now he would be drinking his meals from a straw for the rest of his life. I pushed all of my power into halting the spell and was rewarded by the decay stopping before it reached his chest and head.

I fell away from the brawler and landed on my office floor as a flood of nausea came over me.

My head was swimming with the power of the void. Too long under its influence can drive a person mad, and I had faced enough brushes with madness in my life to know better. Pushing all of that power from my mind took an intense amount of focus. When it was finally gone, I got to my feet and looked to Nancy.

"It looks worse than it is," I lied. "I got us answers, though. They are with the Traum Kult, but that's not what they are calling themselves anymore."

Nancy's dazed and distressed look seemed to abate a little as she asked, "What are they calling themselves?"

The cultist was whimpering on the floor. "I didn't get that far in my questions. They don't know what's going on outside, though."

"What now?"

I drew my gun and headed toward the door, leaving Carol and the witch tied in their respective seats.

"We do our jobs and defend this campus."

Sea of the Dead

We were through the halls and back into the streets just in time to see Jack shift from a vaguely human form into a gross mass of limbs and tentacles. He was killing dozens of the undead at a time with tentacles and jaws that seemed to grow from nothing and looked as though they belonged to creatures that shouldn't exist.

Private Ruddel and Sergeant Neil were standing just behind their monster and doing their best to keep the corpses from overwhelming them. In the time since we had left, the mission had turned from stopping the things from reaching the school to just staying alive. The USEC representatives had created a mountain of bodies from their victories but the number of undead still marching toward them seemed to have doubled while we had been interrogating the cultist.

Between the exit of Miskatonic's administrative building and the soldiers were at least a hundred of the dead.

"What's the plan?" Nancy raised her machine gun and aimed it toward the approaching reanimated.

My sword cleared the sheath on my belt, and I put the pistol back into its holster. I aimed the black blade at the nearest enemy and answered, "Get to Neil."

"That's it?" Nancy sounded unsure. "I was hoping you'd have something a little more powerful to suggest."

I didn't like the feeling that had washed over me or the look that Nancy had given me when I touched the veil to conduct my interview. The power had been intoxicating, but her look had been a mirror into what I could become.

Killing monsters did no good if I became one in the process.

"That's only the first part of the plan," I answered. "I'll let you know when I come up with part two."

I took the first step down the stairs of the administrative building and brought my sword across the chest of the first dead thing that came at me. It fell back as a wound opened in its dried chest, making room for the next to lunge forward. My sword swung through the air in a constant and fluid movement, never halting as I cut the dead monsters down. Even over the rush of battle, I could make out the regular staccato of Nancy's machine gun as she pushed them away from our sides.

When I reached the fifth or sixth one in my path, I noticed that one of them had a slash across his chest. It was the first one that I had attacked in my march toward Sergeant Neil and the USEC. Faltering as I noticed that it was still standing, I only barely avoided its gnashing teeth as they tried to clamp into my wrist. Stepping back, I pulled my wrist out of its grasp and kicked it in the chest before stepping forward and skewering its head with my sword. This time it went down.

It only took me a quick glance over my shoulder to confirm what I had feared. The magic in my sword, which normally destroyed anything touched by the void, wasn't working on these things. Nancy was being forced to put down the dead that my sword wasn't killing.

Why wasn't my sword's magic working on these monsters?

There was no time to contemplate what that meant. The streets were flooded with the undead and we needed to reach the sergeant before they were overwhelmed while not getting overwhelmed ourselves.

My next swipe took the heads off of two of them, and I spun and punched another in the chest to knock them back. I pulled my fist back, covered in my own blood, and noticed that the one I had punched was wearing Nazi medals on an officer's uniform. After impaling his head, I scanned the nearest to me and saw a mix of clothing styles that didn't make sense. There were the nondescript articles of the French Resistance, several more Nazi dress uniforms, cult clothing from the Yig followers, and several tribal headdresses that I wouldn't have expected to see anywhere other than in small island communities. None of them were anything that the dead of Arkham, Massachusetts would be wearing.

Three monsters converged on me and I halted. Nancy crashed into me from behind and we were back-to-back as still more must have crowded us from behind.

Thrusting out, I pierced the nearest undead; she was wearing the tattered remains of a ball gown that was about thirty years out of date. My blade went through her shoulder and I pulled her closer to put her between me and the other two, a man dressed in rancher's gear and another in a German uniform. I swung her left and right as I pushed them back into the crowd that was forming in their uncoordinated effort to eat Nancy and me. I pulled the sword out in an arc, cutting a large chunk out of the ballroom dancer. At the same time, I kicked out and destroyed the knee of the Nazi. My sword never stopped, and I brought it down and into the Nazi's skull and just as quickly pulled it back out, slamming the hilt into the dancer's head, re-killing her.

Even with Nancy at my back and shooting every beast that came within grabbing range of us, we were still getting overrun by them. I thrust out my sword, taking another in the face as I drew my pistol with my off-hand and shot two more that were snapping their jaws too close to be ignored.

As we advanced, we were slowed further by the returned corpses littering the street. In the back of my mind, I realized that my pistol was also facing the same issues as my sword and was only working on the animated dead as well as any other pistol would have done.

Suddenly a tentacle burst through the nearest undead's head and snaked around me, impaling the skulls of six more undead before retreating and letting the corpses drop to the ground.

Jack stood on the other side of the fallen corpses and didn't spare me or Nancy a glance as he cleared a path for us to Sergeant Neil and Private Ruddel. I repressed a shudder, thinking of how close this shoggoth was to me, and resisted the urge to try my sword's magic on him. He was an ally today, even if I didn't believe it for a second.

"Glad you could join us," Neil barked over the volume of the guns.

"For whatever good it'll do," I answered. "We need to retreat. This isn't a battle that we can win."

The sergeant agreed. "Retreat to where?"

I hated saying it, knowing that it meant I was breaking my only rule with the USEC, but there was no other option.

"To the campus. The school's protections should buy us enough time to figure out our next step."

Nancy sighed as she stopped firing into the crowd. "We have to go through that mess again?"

I shrugged and waved at Jack. "Can he make us a path?"

Sergeant Neil nodded. "If we move quickly. He could get overwhelmed in a matter of seconds. We will need to move fast."

Neil gave the order, shouting it so that Jack could hear, and we moved to the edge of the small circle the two soldiers had been holding and waited. As soon as the order was given Jack melted, turning fluid and falling to the pavement. He disappeared from sight for an uncomfortable length of time before he reconstituted himself between us and the administrative building.

His body rippled and then surged toward us and the facility. The thing that pretended to be human turned into a giant length of glistening flesh as the undead bounced away from it or were consumed by the snapping jaws and pincers that appeared all along its edge. Just as quickly as the meat log had formed, it pulsed again and was returned to the semi-human shape of Jack. He whipped his tentacles around to keep the monsters that had been knocked back at bay before shouting, "Now. Hurry."

Jack wasn't a perfect fighting machine and we found ourselves fighting as we ran. I never took the time to reload my pistol, so I kept stabbing while Nancy, Sergeant Neil, and Private Ruddel continued firing into the crowd.

Faster than our entrance into the battle had been, we made our way back into the building and slammed the doors shut. I collapsed on the floor with my back against the door and took in deep breaths.

"Shouldn't we barricade the door?" Tim demanded.

I shook my head and hooked my thumb over my shoulder. "The building's warding starts at the stairs. They can't climb them without significant difficulty, and by the time they get to the door they'll be dust." Standing, I added, "The buildings of this campus only let living and breathing human beings in, but those wards won't last forever. They were never meant to stand up to this level of onslaught."

Ignoring me, Jack stepped forward and pressed his immense strength against the doors.

The sergeant's face was concentrating on a distant thought, and I could see a hint of fear that seemed foreign on the face of the USEC commander.

Tim didn't keep his thoughts quiet. "What are we going to do now?" He waved his hand at the door, "There are so many of them. We've never seen that many before."

"We stay calm," his sergeant answered. "We remember our training and come up with a strategy."

It sent an involuntary shudder down my spine when I heard my own words to Nancy, mirrored almost exactly, coming from the sergeant's lips. It forced me to see more similarities between this commander of men and my own crusade against the dark. I wasn't sure how I felt about that.

"Suggestions, Doran?" Sergeant Neil had turned his attention to me as I became lost in thought.

"The private is right," I agreed. "There are too many of them and they are in too decent a condition to be from Arkham."

"What do you mean?" Neil asked.

Nancy answered for me. "None of them are … goopy. They are either mummified and dried out or they are fresh enough that they almost look alive. Either way, there's no in-between. There should at least be some of them with their oozing bits all over the place."

She had hit the nail on the head, and I picked up where my assistant had left off.

"There's something strange going on here, and it's stranger than a swarm of the dead attacking our campus." Neil's face flashed confusion again as I spoke. "What are you thinking, Sergeant?" I pressed.

Hearing his rank addressed brought Neil's attention back to the here and now.

"What?"

I sighed. "I can't imagine that in all your time with the USEC this is the first you've seen dead things walking around. So, what did you see that has you so distracted?"

Neil's face turned red. "It was nothing."

"Listen up, folks," I raised my voice even though I didn't need to. "We are all aware of the type of world that we're fighting and how insane it can make us. That being said, everything is relevant until it isn't." I refocused my attention on the sergeant. "What did you see?"

"Scott Warren." He said it so quietly, I almost wasn't certain I had heard anything.

"Scott Warren?" I repeated. "Who is Scott Warren?"

Private Ruddel's mouth fell open and Jack's eyes, looking more human than I had seen previously, bore down on his commanding officer.

While still staring at Sergeant Neil, Jack explained, "Ensign Scott Warren died two years ago. In Northern Ireland. He was burned to ash there."

"You don't think I know that?" Neil barked at the half-beast. "I was the one who lit his pyre. I can't explain it, but it was him."

Nodding, I turned to Nancy. "What did you notice about the dead things? Give me the oddest thing that you can think of that stood out."

Nancy thought it over for only a moment before saying, "Their clothing."

"What about it?" I wanted to see if she noticed what I had.

"There was nothing consistent about it, it wasn't just the different times but also the types of clothing. The clothing seemed to be from all over the world."

Neil, still red in the face, shrugged. "Maybe someone has been collecting them and storing them just for some old wizard to animate and set loose."

"That's a good theory," I allowed, "except I saw the religious headdress of the Ulthar tribe of the Egyptian plains."

Ruddel frowned. "So?"

"So," I answered, "I'm the only living person to have ever found the lost Ulthar tribe."

Sergeant Neil smirked. "Obviously not."

I chose not to argue with the sergeant, although I knew that he was wrong. There was no possible means for anyone else to find the feline worshippers. Not in this century, anyway.

"Jack, step away from the door," I ordered. I tried to keep my distaste in dealing with the creature from my voice. As far as I could tell, I had succeeded, but Jack's impassive emotions did little to confirm or deny my efforts.

"Legion of the dead outside," Nancy grabbed my arm. "That's probably a bad idea."

Yanking my arm from her grasp, I countered, "I'm only going to take a peek. If they are still out there, Jack can slam his supernatural mass into the doors and keep us safe. Besides," I waved Jack out of the way, "even with Jack and the school's wards, that many dead things should have been able to make it in here by now."

"What?" Everyone shouted in unison.

Ignoring them, I yanked open the double doors.

Students looked up at where my companions and I were standing, and staring, out into the street. Cars were moving up and down the street while the day progressed in much the same manner that it did every day.

The sun was shining and there wasn't a dead thing in sight.

"Where did they go?" Nancy asked as she lowered her gun.

"That's the point that I think the doctor was trying to get across," Sergeant Neil answered. "They were never there."

"But our guns…" Tim's voice was barely a whisper.

I pulled the doors shut again and turned to the cadre of soldiers I'd assembled, Nancy included. "I don't know how it all works, but it might be less that they weren't here and more that we weren't."

"What?" Jack muttered.

"Whatever happened," I attempted a poor explanation, "illusions were formed from images in our mind by an outside influence. As for why the streets aren't shot to hell by our behavior in reaction to those illusions, I don't know. It could be that instead of generating this illusion in our minds, it actually created it in a nearby pocket of reality. At some point, we stepped out of our reality and into this pocket dimension. The illusion disappeared when the energies powering the pocket dimension were stopped."

"But you don't know?" Tim asked.

I shook my head. "I'm guessing, and to be completely honest, it doesn't change anything. The only thing that we know for certain is that someone is messing with us."

"How do we know that?" Sergeant Neil asked.

Nancy took her turn and tried explaining. "We've been targeted, for whatever reason. Something put only us into an illusion filled with things that only we had seen before. It could have had us shooting up the streets of Arkham, but instead it just wanted us afraid. That implies structured thought and an agenda."

Neil nodded, impressed not for the first time by Nancy's sharp mind.

"Could it have been the Traum Kult?" I asked, wondering what the USEC might know about the cultists being in my school.

"The Traum Kult?" Private Ruddel's face wrinkled in disgust. "What do those Nazi bastards have to do with any of this?"

Nancy hooked her thumb in my direction. "We found three of them outside of Andy's office. They picked a fight. One of them is dead, but the other two..." Nancy cast a sidelong glance at me that hinted at her distaste in what I'd had to do earlier, "... are subdued."

The sergeant's face grew red, as he found something that he could fight. "If the Traum Kult are here, then you should have told us immediately. They are an enemy of the United States and a potential intelligence asset against the Reich."

The sergeant's ire only agitated my own. "Calm down," I barked. "We did come straight to you, but you were a little busy with the illusionary dead. We still have one who is in perfect health that you can interrogate." I started to turn toward my office to lead the way before I realized that there was more on my mind. Spinning around, I stopped almost nose to nose with the sergeant.

"If you ever try to pull rank on me or my people again, try

to remember where you're standing. No matter what the United States Esoteric Calvary has faced, they've always bowed to the wisdom of Miskatonic University and its dean." I took a breath before adding, "That's because Miskatonic keeps the USEC's nightmares in our 101 courses."

To Neil's credit, he never flinched. "Watch your tone, Doctor. There have been more than a few requests to add your name to the list of wizards and monsters that the USEC hunts. We are currently at war and you would do well to remember which side you are fighting for."

"We're on the side that eliminates monsters, not the one that uses them," Nancy came to my defense.

"Jack just saved our lives," Tim countered.

I pulled away from the sergeant. "Are we going to fight, or figure out what happened?"

Everyone got quiet as if waiting for a decision to be made, so I made it for them and pushed open the nearest door.

It opened into one of the standard lecture rooms.

"Shouldn't we be headed to your office?" Neil asked.

"I have another theory that should be shared before we're in a room with potential enemies."

When the door shut, I continued.

"This might be the work of the Scroll of Eibon. I don't know how, but I think it has something to do with all of this."

Nancy frowned, obviously disagreeing. "Weird stuff happens all of the time. Why would any of the new weird stuff have anything to do with the scroll?" She trailed off before following my logic. "Unless … Do you think that what happened to Carol is part of this, too?"

I nodded. "Reanimated corpses are scary to anyone, and the Ulthar Tribes are a memory from a very dark time in my past." I turned and waved to the private. "And I'm sure that whoever Scott Warren is, he haunts you."

Sergeant Neil held up his hands. "Who's Carol, and what happened to her?"

"Carol is our wendigo secretary, domesticated and very proud of it for almost a century. Wendigo are connected to Hyperborea, the same place that powers whatever spells are written on the scroll. When we brought it on campus, Carol went feral and tried to get to it."

Private Ruddel nodded. "That makes sense. The similar magics called to each other. The USEC has seen this kind of thing before." He frowned. "That doesn't cause illusions of the dead, though."

Nodding again, I continued, "Unless we consider what might scare a woman who has fought her darker nature for over a century."

"She's afraid of losing control." Nancy's voice was barely audible.

I nodded and added to Nancy's thought, "And the moment that we brought the scroll near her, her worst fears came true." I couldn't help but cast a glance in Jack's direction.

Neil smirked. "Are you suggesting that the scroll is making our fears into reality?"

"It's a guess," I answered, "and one I wouldn't have even made if I hadn't seen the reanimated Ulthar tribesman."

"Why is it only affecting us?" the sergeant asked.

I shrugged. "It might still have a consciousness, and that consciousness spent days in a plane with only the group that is right here. It might have needed that time and proximity to make a mental connection."

"But we're guessing." Nancy killed the theoretical discussion where it was. "We don't actually know anything more than illusions are being controlled by someone or something and that they might be connected to the Traum Kult or to Hyperborea."

"Or to both," the sergeant added. "It all seems like quite the stretch of the imagination."

Nancy sighed, obviously getting tired of the USEC leader. "Let's hope so. I find it hard to believe that Carol is the only monster afraid of losing control." She gave a slight nod to Jack.

Neil straightened up. "You can all push that from your minds right this instant."

"What's the plan, sir?" Private Ruddel seemed eager to move on as well.

The sergeant waved in my general direction. "Assuming that our gracious host doesn't object, the plan is to stay on campus.

Whether it's the scroll or not, the creatures were headed this way. With the Traum Kult here as well, the intelligent course of action would be to use Miskatonic University as our temporary base of operations. From here we can interrogate the Traum Kult captives and provide any defense that the school might require."

Everyone stared at me, awaiting my approval. I took a moment to say anything, hoping that the sergeant was aware of the shift in power and immediately admonished myself for it. We were on the same team after all, and it wouldn't do me any good to keep fighting with him over anything.

"Welcome to Miskatonic University," I answered with less luster in my voice than I had attempted.

Green Lazarus

Our initial theorizing done, we raced back to my office. Not much had changed in mine and Nancy's absence. The woman from the Traum Kult was awake, as was Carol. Both were thankfully still bound where we had left them. The former Traum Kult brawler on the other hand took a moment to locate. In his damaged state he had taken to crawling under my desk for a nap.

As we entered the office, Carol's eyes went wide and zeroed in on Private Tim Ruddel instantly.

"He's bleeding," I snapped as realization dawned. "Move him to the other side of the room and find out where and how bad. Let's get him bandaged so my secretary can stop drooling."

Sergeant Neil pulled a small package from his pack and tossed it to Nancy as she guided Tim around my snarling friend and to the other side of my large office. I've never been as gaudy as my predecessors, but was appreciative of the excess of space provided for the dean's office.

I started toward Carol to check on her when Sergeant Neil grabbed my arm. There was no force in it, so I didn't react as if there was. He simply had a concern.

"We should collect the scroll and move it someplace secure."

My head shook at the notion. "There's no place safer than where it already is. It stays put for now."

It was obvious that he didn't like that idea, but he also knew when to play the stern hand and when to back down. Releasing my arm, he went about checking on his men and surveying the Traum Kult members scattered around my office.

"How are you feeling?" I asked Carol when the sergeant was out of earshot.

While Carol's face was still the pale shade of her wendigo side, her body was entirely human looking. That was a marked improvement over when I had been forced to knock her out.

"I'm at odds," she said slowly. Her voice had a quiet growl behind each of the words that most people wouldn't notice. I was looking for it, though, and picked it up immediately. "I equally do and do not want to kill you."

"Sounds like you're back to normal?" I smiled at her as I checked her bonds. "Is there anything that I can do to help?"

Carol's smile showed teeth that were still not entirely human. "Untie me and run?" Shaking her head, she took a few deep breaths. "Sorry. Unless you know how to block the influence of the scroll on me, then no." She swallowed hard. "You should keep me bound. Perhaps bind me even tighter."

"Are you one hundred percent certain that it's the scroll and not something else?" I asked.

Carol gave me an incredulous look. "Are you joking?" When she saw that I wasn't, she continued. "It's the scroll. Without a doubt." She saw something in my eye. "Why? What else happened?"

I gave her the quick recap of what had happened outside and our discovery that it was an illusion aimed only at us.

"Hyperborea is the home of many dream magics." Her voice was almost wistful. "It wouldn't be a stretch for someone from there to push into your minds." She frowned. "I don't know that an inanimate object can have that effect."

"I'm beginning to think that there's more to that scroll than just being an inanimate object," I replied. An idea suddenly came to my mind on how we might be able to help Carol block the influence of the scroll.

"Hold that thought" I said, and darted over to where Neil was interrogating the Traum Kult witch.

Ignoring the sergeant's line of questioning, I interrupted. "What do you know about Hyperborean magic?"

The witch looked up at me with annoyance. "Like I was telling your boss, I'm not telling any of you anything."

Folding my arms, I leaned a little closer to the witch.

"You know who I am and what I am. I know that you have

been briefed on my life story. Do you really think that," I hooked my thumb at Sergeant Neil, "he's in charge?" I didn't wait for her to answer. Pointing at the desk where her companion was still snoring and drooling on my rug, I continued, "I'm also the guy that did that to your friend. If you want to still be you in the next ten minutes, then I suggest that you start cooperating." I took a deep breath to let that sink in before repeating, "What do you know about Hyperborean magic?"

The sergeant was obviously annoyed with me, but he wasn't going to ruin a potential intelligence asset over some tough words. He kept his lips tight and waited to see what the witch said.

"I'm physically incapable of sharing any information regarding the Traum Kult." Her voice was quiet, but I could still make it out. "There are protections in place that make it impossible."

"I don't care about the Traum Kult," I replied. "Hyperborean magic. Everything."

The witch nodded. "I don't know a lot, but I know enough to tell you that this place is soaked in it."

I leaned against my desk and relaxed my posture a little. "What's your name?"

"I'm enrolled as Mae Cunningham."

"Mae," I kept my voice calm, "I have a problem. You're right, of course. This place is saturated in the type of magic that comes from the world of Hyperborea. We're swimming in it. This wouldn't normally be a problem, because we're all mostly human…"

"But you have a wendigo on the payroll," Mae finished for me. She threw a glance over her shoulder to look at Carol. "How many did she kill?"

"Nobody yet," I answered, "but we don't want her to kill anyone. To that point, do you know of anything we can do to …" I wasn't certain how to word it, " … filter some of that magic from affecting her?"

Mae shrugged. "She's directly connected to it. You can't stop it from touching her without destroying her."

I had expected as much. "We don't want to break her

connection to that frozen world. We just want to weaken it."

Her furrowed brow showed that she was putting some effort behind the problem. "There's a spell that was made by an Indian tribe in Canada. Wendigo had become a problem, so they branded this spell into the backs of all of their people. It made it impossible for them to be affected by Hyperborea's touch if they were in a position where they would normally turn." The witch was obviously referencing the starvation and cannibalism that were the hallmarks of that change.

"I just said that we didn't want to block the connection," I said. "That's exactly what that sounds like we'd be doing."

Mae shook her head. "It's possible that you could adjust the spell so that it's weaker than the original. A tattoo instead of a brand, or alter the language so that it doesn't break the connection."

"Do you know this spell?" I asked.

Mae nodded.

I couldn't halt my curiosity. "Why? What does the Traum Kult need with a spell that blocks Hyperborean magic?"

Her face twisted with anger and annoyance. "I told you that I can't speak to my relationship with the Traum Kult, but I'm sure you can figure out why someone positioned at Miskatonic University with a false identity might need to know how to neutralize beings of Hyperborean influence."

I nodded. She had already shown herself to be aware that my secretary was a wendigo. If she had been placed here to watch me, then she was fully aware that taking me out, if that is what she was ordered to do, could mean a fight with my associates.

"How do I know that any spell you provided me with wouldn't kill her or make her connection stronger?"

She shrugged again. "You're going to decide how to edit a spell you know nothing about. It could kill her. I can't help that, and you'll probably kill me for it, anyway. As for it making her stronger, that wouldn't help me at all. If I make her stronger, she will kill us all, but she'll start with me first." Mae tugged against her bindings to emphasize how helpless she was.

Freeing one of Mae's hands, I moved her closer to the desk and gave her a pad of paper and a pencil.

"Write down what we need to do. If this works you might make it back to your bosses alive and sane."

Mae doubted my words, but obviously couldn't find an alternative and began scribbling on the page.

Nancy was finished bandaging up Ruddel when I noticed the private trying to discreetly look her up and down. The sudden surge of emotion caught me by surprise. Nancy was entirely oblivious to both Ruddel's attention and my flash of jealousy, and I intended to keep it that way.

The normally hyper-observant assistant of mine was oblivious only because something inside Sergeant Neil's medical bag had caught her eye. While she didn't have a medical background by any measure, Nancy wasn't one to be distracted by things of a normal nature.

Reaching in, my assistant brought out a leather pouch that she immediately set to opening. There was a large syringe with a cap over the needle and two vials of a glowing green substance. Nancy held up one of the glowing vials for closer inspection.

Without taking my eyes off of the bottle in Nancy's hand, I addressed the sergeant. "Is that what I think it is?"

Neil stomped forward, almost violently grabbed the bottle from Nancy's hand, and set about returning it and the leather case back to his medical bag.

"If I can save one life in the field," the sergeant said as an answer, "against the monsters that the USEC has faced, then I will do so at all costs."

"What is it?" Nancy's question was directed at me.

"That," I explained, "is a serum developed during the Great War for making the dead into monsters like what we were just facing."

"Wrong." Neil's voice wasn't entirely a shout, but it was close enough. "The Green Lazarus formula has been through 20 years of refinement. It now has a 95% success rate at reversing fatal wounds and reviving the dead entirely to their previous states."

My eyes went wide with surprise. The formula, as I previously understood it, was more likely to cause insanity to anyone it revived. It would drive them mad with their reversed state and cause them to become homicidal monsters. During the early 1920s, Arkham had been the epicenter for countless murders committed by the creatures that elixir created. If the sergeant was telling the truth, this new solution would be entirely different from the original, and potentially a boon for society as a whole.

I couldn't help myself in my curiosity. "What about the 5%?"

Tim Ruddel was the one who answered my question. "They still become psychotic monsters."

Nodding, I understood the sympathy in his voice. He'd seen it happen.

"Still," I admitted, "Ninety-five percent is an incredible achievement. Perfectly acceptable in an emergency situation, if not necessarily for public use." Smirking, I added, "Green Lazarus? I like the name. It's better than anything that the original creator tried to call it."

Nancy finally realized what we were talking about and asked, "Are you saying that this serum cures death?"

The private was excited by her interest and answered with a large smile across his face. "Yes, exactly."

"How did you get past the initial problems?" I asked Neil. "The instability decay?"

The sergeant shrugged. "I'm a grunt. I don't know the science specifics, but my understanding is that most of those instabilities were a direct result of a personality flaw in the original doctor. Once we replaced that maniac with some of America's top scientists, success was easier to achieve."

Mae held up the pad of paper with her freed hand. I took it from her and started toward Carol.

As I moved, Neil grabbed my arm.

"Are you sure we have time for this?" he asked. "Traum Kult are on your campus and the dead are at your doors."

I ignored how obviously wrong he was in the latter half of his statement. The dead weren't at our doors so much as an illusion was in our mind, but this wasn't the time for semantics.

I yanked my arm free from his grasp and growled, "You've got your monster, I need mine."

"About that," Neil smirked. "You're quite the hypocrite

condemning us for working with a monster when you do the same damn thing."

"My monster is a person who's been victimized by magic while yours is an alien abomination developed by interdimensional scientists with the sole purpose of killing as many people as possible." I shook my head. "I give people the benefit of the doubt. Not monsters."

To the sergeant's credit, he kept his mouth shut and didn't stop me as I moved toward my administrative assistant.

As I reached her, the phone rang and Nancy answered it. After a brief exchange she hung it up and turned to me.

"Things just got worse," she explained. "The dead are back and we're no longer the only ones seeing them."

"This is going to cause a panic," the sergeant said in a whisper.

"That's not all," Nancy continued. "There's an invisible thing attacking the students in the main quad. They are calling it an invisible tiger. Students say they just saw a janitor float into the air before he was torn to pieces by an unseen force."

Behind me, in a thick French accent, a sultry voice whispered, "Your world is being torn apart."

I ignored the voice and turned back to Carol. "We need to work fast."

The sergeant was on the move. "Agreed. We'll hunt the creature. Join us when your team is ready."

I agreed and the USEC left my office.

Turning to Carol, I asked, "What are your thoughts on tattoos?"

Distraction in the Library

Tattooing isn't an art normally associated with the deans of prestigious universities. To my credit, I had never wanted the job anyway. Travel with enough cultures and outcast occult societies long enough and you have little choice but to learn how to tattoo. Some spells, both of defense and offense, required the permanent art of ink on skin.

To Carol's credit, she never questioned my credentials or what it was that I was attempting to do. I could have dismissed that as her being too preoccupied by her current set of circumstances, but decided it was more likely her incredible confidence in me and what I could do.

Even I laughed at that thought.

My skills weren't great, but I could follow Mae's instructions well enough. I wasn't just altering the spell that the witch had suggested but I actually recognized the majority of the symbols and their meanings from my time studying the Necronomicon. Using my knowledge from that forbidden text, I changed the meaning of the tattoo from "break the connection" to "weaken the connection."

Even so, I could not be entirely certain that the tattoo was correct. The mixture of ancient symbols from the Necronomicon with the entirely foreign symbols of Hyperborean magic left me hopeful at best. For good measure, I tattooed the spell on both of her wrists and her upper back, using ink from one of my desk pens and a method I had learned from a Yig princess I once traveled with. Perhaps the combination of the three spells across her body would weaken the connection enough for Carol to resume her duties, both administrative and militant.

When I was done, I called Nancy over to aim a pistol at Carol while I cut her bonds.

Once that was done, Nancy and I backed out of the room, leaving Carol with Mae.

The witch's fear became evident quickly. "What are you doing?"

I smiled as I shut the door. "Making certain that you didn't lie to us."

As the door clicked and the wards fell into place, Nancy and I patiently waited a full five minutes.

The screams never came. Instead, Nancy and I could hear the shuffling of the chair Mae had been tied to as she tried to put some distance between herself and the flesh-eating monster. When the five minutes were finally up, Carol came to the door and called out.

"All is clear. You can come back in."

Carol's flesh had started to regain its pink and more human color.

"How are you feeling?" Nancy asked.

"Much better," Carol answered, "but I can still feel the pull of the scroll. It's just more..." she paused as she looked for the word, "distant."

"Good," I said. "We've got a campus to save."

As we started toward the door, the Traum Kult witch called out to us. "What about me?"

"Oh right," I answered and ran back over to her. Once her hand was tied again to the chair, we locked the office and took off after the USEC.

As we rounded the corner, we heard the students screaming about the dead in the streets.

Whatever had been creating these illusions had decided to pull out all the stops and had started including the students in the illusions as well.

"What do we do about that?" Nancy asked. "They said they are beating on the doors."

"Stick to the plan and join the soldiers," was the only thing I could think to say. "They might already have something in the works for the fictional dead."

Having Carol at my back again was both a relief and a concern. While it was great to have such a competent warrior and friend at my side, it was hard to forget the hungry look in her eyes as she tore a path across the armory. As with many times in the past, I had to push my reservations regarding this ally to the side for the greater good. My only hope was that her bestial nature wasn't capable of planning a convincing surprise attack.

We rounded the corner of the hall and came to an abrupt halt in the library as Nancy stumbled over the unconscious form of Private Ruddel. Only a foot away from the downed soldier was Sergeant Neil. His machine gun fired in bursts at what looked to be nothing, but I knew better than to take the image before me at face value.

Aside from the bullets not hitting any of the walls or bookshelves that they were aimed at, there was also the obviously distressed form of Jack suspended in mid-air.

He was wrestling with something that presumably had been the target of the sergeant's gunfire. Jack's limbs had formed into tentacles that sliced and grabbed at the beast that held him. One tentacle swung about and fired a machine gun directly into the invisible mass to seemingly no effect.

Reaching into the void and drawing on the power from beyond the veil, I allowed myself to look into the world and see what was holding the shoggoth-soldier hybrid.

Normally, I would have been surprised by what I saw, but this had been a day of disappointments. Where there should have been an un-nameable thing that we couldn't see because our brains simply couldn't comprehend its many dimensions, there was instead nothing.

The other thing I saw was Jack. His shoggoth body was a dark mass of terrifying vitriol but that wasn't all he was. In his center mass was a glowing thing that I could only describe as an unearthly shade of blue. It was the human presence within. Perhaps the light was the actual brain of Jack himself.

"It's another illusion," I shouted over the barking gunfire. "Probably pulled from my mind."

"You've fought something like this before?" Nancy asked.

I nodded. "In Berlin. The monster's extradimensional properties meant that the mind couldn't comprehend it, making it essentially invisible. At the time, I could look through the void and make it out, but when I do that here nothing happens. Nothing is actually there."

"What do you want me to do?" Carol asked. To anyone still in the library who didn't know her true potential, it would have been an odd thing to see the middle-aged woman rolling up her sleeves and preparing for battle.

"Don't go full wendigo," I said. "We don't need to risk a problem." With a nod, she ran at the phantasm and leapt.

I turned to Neil and he stopped firing.

"Guns aren't working," I hooked my thumb at Jack, "and neither is he. Head to the front and keep the dead out of my school."

Sergeant Neil seemed confused. "The dead? They're back?"

I gave a quick nod. "They appeared shortly after this guy did. Whoever is running this show wants our full attention."

The sergeant scooped up Ruddel from the ground.

"We'll take him with us," he explained. "Stay alive."

When Jack hit the ground again, the sergeant yelled his order and they retreated toward the front doors of Miskatonic's administrative building. It caught my attention that Jack didn't hesitate to leave the situation. The speed with which he reacted to his commander's orders seemed less a reaction from his military background and more of something else.

Or I was letting my paranoia get the best of me.

I drew my pistol and fired three rounds into where I was sure the beast was still standing. Loud and unearthly groans echoed from it as Carol took another leap at it.

Nancy began a volley of her own from her machine gun, letting up only to let Carol try for another personal strike.

My frustration was beginning to get the better of me. We couldn't win a fight against a creature of imagination without taking out the beast causing it. We were going to be fighting this thing until it exhausted and overwhelmed us, and that wasn't a scenario that I had any plans for.

Suddenly, it occurred to me that you couldn't fight an

imaginary undead horde either. Both were just physical assaults meant to keep us wasting our time.

For what reason, though?

"It's a distraction," I shouted at my companions.

Nancy glanced at me while she let loose with another round of gunfire. "For the scroll? How many distractions do we need in one day for someone to actually grab it?" She let out a loud sigh. "This is getting ridiculous."

"The Traum Kult, the USEC, and even Carol have all gone off the rails in one way or another as they tried to get that scroll," I explained. "Whoever it is can't get to it themselves and are using these illusions to buy themselves time to get to it."

The blood on the library floor reminded me that illusions or not, these creatures were hurting people. I didn't know whether to stay and keep the students and staff safe, or run for the scroll. In the end, the decision was clear. We could fight the symptoms all day, but it would not do if the disease continued to run its course.

"I wish we knew who was doing this," Nancy shouted.

"It doesn't matter," was my reply. "The goal is the same."

"Can anyone get into the armory?" Carol asked as she caught her breath. The invisible monster slammed an appendage through a set of bookshelves, turning them to splinters.

I wanted to say no, but I wasn't entirely sure that someone with enough power and time at their disposal wouldn't be able to.

A soft breath tickled my ear and the voice with the French accent was speaking to me again. "Anyone that has the power to get into your head has the power to get into the armory."

Spinning around, I held my pistol aimed at her chest. It was impossible. She couldn't be here. She had died on two planes of existence. There was no bringing her back.

"You're not here," I said to Olivia, the phantasm that resided in my shattered mind for the better part of two years. "You're dead."

Olivia pointed in the general direction of the invisible monster. "So is that thing. That is the beast that tore apart Abdul Alhazred in the marketplace thousands of years ago."

She grinned from ear to ear. "So, tell me why it is here."

It was so hard to think with her standing there. Olivia represented everything that I feared; she was the worst parts of me. Power-hungry and craving control over my physical form, she was the monster version of myself. Illusion or not, I was terrified.

She was helping me, though. Reminding me that the monster was fake and therefore so was she. Both taken from the depths of my mind to torment us.

"Why are you here?"

"Sorry, love," she replied. "I can only torment you with half-truths."

She dove at me and grabbed the sides of my head.

"Now let me back inside."

Return to the Armory

Stars of pain lanced through my entire body. The pain didn't stop at my head, as Olivia was trying to take over my entire self. I couldn't see clearly; my vision filled with shades of red and bright light. Through it all, I could feel her fingers as they sunk into the flesh and burrowed through my mind.

As much as it hurt, I am no stranger to pain and learned a long time ago that there is always a weapon in my arsenal for fighting past it.

I let the fear take me. It was the fear that Olivia wasn't actually a dream created by whatever thing was after the Scroll of Eibon. I tasted the fear that she was standing in front of me, somehow alive again or perhaps never dead, and capable of climbing back into my skull. I pushed back with all of the strength that my fear gave me, knowing how futile the effort was.

Olivia and the pain were suddenly gone.

I fell to the ground gasping and panting as I clutched at my temples where her fingers had been boring in.

As my senses came back under my control, I could hear Nancy screaming in rage.

"You killed my father," she gasped between her screams. I looked up and saw her straddling Olivia, punching my psychosis repeatedly. She wasn't wrong in her fury. When I had first removed Olivia from my mind I hadn't killed her, but had instead traded her to a creature in the Dream Lands. It wasn't my best moment, but it was the only way to get her out of my mind that I could find. When she had escaped her new prison, she'd learned how to take over the bodies of those who slept and used that power to kill William Dyer, Nancy's father, with Nancy's own possessed form.

Carol took that moment to crash through another set of bookshelves. Blood covered her face as she stood and ran back at the invisible thing that had supposedly killed the author of the Necronomicon all those years ago. All of the wounds on her body didn't slow her at all as she leapt fifteen or more feet into the air to jump on the creature.

Nancy finally surrendered her punching efforts and grabbed her machine gun. Swinging it around she pressed it to Olivia's head and pulled the trigger. Olivia vanished and the floor erupted in chunks of tile.

Olivia's disappearance must have triggered something in their real enemy, as Carol fell through the air where her foe had been only seconds ago. It had dissolved along with Olivia.

"Monsters from our minds." I was shouting louder than intended as I waited for the last of the ringing in my ears to go away. "Olivia was a monster from my mind and," I pointed over to where Carol sat cross-legged on the floor, "that thing was an ancient beast sent to murder a wizard."

"Distractions?" Nancy asked. She was still panting as her adrenaline hung on.

I nodded. "Yes. Just more distractions."

With all of the monsters gone for at least the moment, we turned and ran in the direction of the armory.

As we ran down the halls, Sergeant Neil came around the corner and joined us. Blood covered his uniform, but it seemed that none of it was his. I couldn't help but wonder where Jack and the private were. "Are you headed to the armory?"

We nodded and I asked, "Why? Do you know something?"

It was his turn to nod. He waved for us to keep moving and we all broke into a run.

Neil didn't start talking right away, so I filled him in on what we had learned.

"They're all distractions, obviously," I said between breaths. "We still can't figure out who or what is causing all of this, but one of the projections told me that if they can get into my head they can probably pull out how to get into the armory."

"I think Jack is somehow involved," Neil said. "He's been having psychic communications with something. When we were fighting the dead out front, he stopped and spoke to someone. Private Ruddel tried to snap him out of it once he was back on his feet..."

I glanced at Neil and saw the grim look on his face.

"Jack tore him apart quicker than I've ever seen him move," he explained.

As little as I knew Timothy Ruddel, it was easy to see that he was a decent soldier and man. His loss angered me, and a quick glance showed me that Nancy was saddened as well.

"The private had warned me that Jack had started talking to himself when we got here," Neil continued, "but I didn't want to believe it." He stopped talking long enough for me to realize that the rest was difficult for him to admit. "I didn't want you to be right."

I didn't care.

"Where is Jack now?" I feared that I already knew the answer.

In unison, Nancy and Sergeant Neil said "The armory."

The front opening to the armory had been hidden behind a large painting of a Brown Jenkin, a creature from the dark corners of the city. It had the body of a rat and the face of a man. I wasn't sure why anyone would have put this picture here other than to avert the gaze of people who would normally pay too much attention to the out-of-place painting.

The painting only served to confirm our fears. It was destroyed, shredded by an unknown force, and lying on the ground. Where it had previously hung was a large hole in the wall that led to the most powerful collection of artifacts that I had knowledge of.

And the Scroll of Eibon.

Everyone stopped and checked their weapons. Nancy changed the drum on her machine gun, Sergeant Neil reloaded his pistols and his rifle, Carol closed her eyes as the nails grew into even longer claws, and I reloaded my pistol before drawing my enchanted sword.

Once we were as ready as we could be for what was beyond the door, we went in.

Our first sign of our adversary was the sound. Loud crashing, shattered glass, howling winds, and noises that no human was capable of describing assaulted our ears. Following the sounds, we found Jack.

Halfway across the armory, Jack was in shoggoth form, not a trace of humanity in any of his amorphous flesh. He was the size of a truck as he rolled through the room. His tentacled arms swung wildly, launching artifacts, tables, and more through the air.

I shot a quick glance at Carol. "Are you good?" I wasn't sure how effective her warding would be this close to the scroll.

Her response was a quick nod and a grunt. I understood that to mean she was struggling but felt that she had it under control. I was going to have to keep an eye on her while we fought.

Stepping forward, I pointed my sword at Jack and shouted a spell that normally sent shoggoths in a pained frenzy.

The beast seemed to barely notice as it turned and we could see that it still retained the face of Jack, buried in the body of the fleshy mass.

"Jack," Neil shouted, "what are you doing?"

Almost faster than the eye could catch, Jack reformed into the dutiful soldier. "Jack no longer exists and has not since you merged us," it explained. "I have only used his mind to give me the tools to fool you and your masters. I do not need him anymore. I have been promised freedom in the new universe."

Jack shuddered and his flesh rippled before a wet mass was ejected from his chest and onto the floor.

"Who promised you?" I asked.

"The prisoner god." Its flesh continued to ripple as it grew back into the mass of flesh and tentacles. "Icthosthau. He has the power to transform this world and he will devour you all."

The shoggoth didn't bother to turn around and instead continued its journey through the armory and toward the scroll.

I started after him, but the sergeant grabbed my arm. "Doran," he had a frantic look on his face, "who the hell is Icthosthau?"

I had been wondering the same thing. "The dialect is

Hyperborean." I let out a sigh. "That place again. I've never heard of a 'prisoner god,' but I'm beginning to think that the Scroll of Eibon is less a book of spells and more … something else."

As with everything related to Hyperborea, I cast my glance to Carol for any sort of answer. Her eyes were closed, and she was mouthing the name over and over again. I was reminded again that I probably shouldn't have brought her this close to the scroll.

When she finally opened her eyes, they were the gray eyes of a wendigo. "Icthosthau is not a prisoner god." Her voice was more bestial, but she seemed to be keeping control over herself. "He was the demon of the ice-torn plains. His power was over fear and dreams. Much as we have experienced, only much worse. He could create entire worlds from strong enough fears. He made nightmares real."

Olivia popped into existence between us all. My entire team jumped, bringing up their weapons and claws.

"Yes," she said, "and he would have ruled over all if not for the wizard, Eibon. He trapped Icthosthau in the scroll and placed it in the space between two worlds, perfectly balanced so that his power could not grab purchase in either." She winked at me and then at Nancy. "That was a perfect prison until the lovebirds pulled it fully into this world and brought it into the presence of beasts that it could bargain with."

She vanished as quickly as she had appeared.

Neil opened fire on Jack just as he reached the glass case holding the scroll. I wasn't worried about a stray bullet hitting the case. It was warded against any attack a human could make. I was more worried about the shoggoth and any attention that it might direct at the case. I didn't know if it could get through it, but I had to assume that it could.

Carol went wide, diving between shelving units as quietly as she could in an effort to get to Jack without him seeing her. It was clear that she had never fought a shoggoth before or she wouldn't have even tried. Shoggoths are unformed masses of flesh with eyes and mouths covering their entire bodies and in random places. There was nothing anyone could do around a shoggoth without being seen by at least one of its many eyes.

Her best hope was for us to distract the shoggoth while she pounced and for that to work, I would need to move fast.

Turning to Nancy, I pointed at the brain on the floor. "Save Jack. That's your priority."

"How do I save Jack?" She was clearly confused. "He's a dead brain on the floor."

I pointed at the large jar with knobs and dials on it that I had discovered earlier that same day. It hadn't been moved in all of the action and still rested only a few tables away. "That is alien technology for reviving and sustaining brains. Put him in the jar and the jar will do the rest."

Disgust contorted Nancy's face. "You mean I have to touch it? The brain?"

I rolled my eyes. "Yes, and we don't have time for this. If you don't put him in that jar soon, he might end up too far gone to save."

Nancy remembered where she was and what we were doing, and her disgust vanished from her face. She ran forward and collected the jar, not slowing as she sprinted toward the brain.

I turned and raised my pistol before firing all six of my magically charged shots into the shoggoth's hide. I was quite satisfied to see darkened spots of dead flesh erupt from where each bullet hit. After an entire day of my weapons having no effect on monsters it was quite nice to see some positive results.

My pistol was reloaded and at my side as I closed distance on the shoggoth. I brought my left arm up and swung my sword at the beast. A tentacle grabbed my sword arm and halted it from having any effect. Before the beast could tear my arm off, I emptied my revolver into it again. Its roar resonated through my body and it threw me across the room.

I landed hard but only a few feet from Nancy and Jack's brain. The second that the brain hit the bottom of the jar, the top of it irised closed and it started filling with a clear liquid. As the brain began to float, cables with needles attached to their ends shot out from the base and penetrated seemingly random places along the surface of the organ.

A voice that sounded vaguely familiar started from the small speaker on the front of the base. It started as grunts and then shifted quickly into an ear-splitting scream.

"Shut up," Nancy covered the speaker with her hands. "Shut up," she repeated. "You're safe for now but there's a damned shoggoth trying to kill us all and your screaming is only going to draw it's attention."

I stood up and walked over to the jar. A quick flip of a switch and the sound coming out of the jar ceased.

"Off switch," I explained to Nancy. "He can still hear you, so try talking to him. He's former Esoteric Calvary, he might be able to handle the truth."

My body hurt everywhere that had hit the ground, but I could see that Carol and Neil weren't faring well against the monster. Every time the shoggoth knocked them away, it would return to beating on the warded glass holding the scroll in place. Even from across the vast armory, I could see cracks forming on its surface. It wouldn't be much longer before the shoggoth broke through.

I sprinted forward and leapt into the air, bringing my sword down into the shoggoth. It let out a piercing scream of pain and I dropped to the ground with my sword still in it.

A swelling in its body happened and then my sword shot out of it and clattered on the floor. Neil fired his machine gun with one hand and his pistol with the other as he tried to damage the monster. Carol tore at the flesh on the opposite side from Neil, ripping large chunks out with her claws that would hit the ground and then slither back to the main body.

A tentacle as fat as a person formed and swung down in an effort to crush me. I rolled to the side and jumped straight in the air as the tentacle tried to follow my movements. It swept under me and stopped as more tentacles branched off and began creating a writhing mass of flesh. I fired into the mass, creating an opening that I could land in. I used the same technique to make myself a path that led directly to my sword.

Casualties

Dripping tentacles darted around me in an attempt to break through my weakening defenses. If Jack had actually still been inside of that monster, the soldier would have known that my gun was down to three bullets. The slight advantage of the shoggoth's driven pursuit to destroy anything trying to stop it from getting to the scroll was the only thing stopping it from making the realization and closing in for the kill.

Raising my pistol, I fired the three shots that emptied my pistol into the mass of flesh between me and my sword. More psychic shrieks of pain erupted in my mind as a hole briefly opened. I dove through it and hit the ground with less grace than I had intended, but I landed directly next to my sword.

Now that the annoying fly that was myself had been removed from the shoggoth's vicinity, it didn't give chase. Instead, it ignored me to refocus its efforts on destroying the magical barriers between it and its prize.

I barked another bit of magic that I knew, and the monster shuddered and collapsed as more screams of agony came out. A wave of nausea and exhaustion came that almost dropped me, too. The spell had taken too much of my energy and I wouldn't be able to use it again. Using the break, I reloaded my pistol and saw Neil doing the same.

"We need to throw everything that we have at it," Neil shouted to me over the monster's wails.

"Haven't we been?" I demanded.

Neil pulled out a grenade. "Almost."

"Don't," I shouted at him. I wasn't sure that the warded glass case could survive a grenade after the pounding it had received from the shoggoth. "It might not even have an effect. Earthly weapons aren't even touching it."

"I'll put it inside of it," he said with a wild grin.

The shoggoth was beginning to rise again and I couldn't use that spell again without taking myself out of the fight.

Carol spoke through panting breaths. "It can hear you, so I don't know how you're planning on pulling that off." She lunged at it before it could return to smashing the case. As she soared through the air, she shifted fully into her wendigo form and resumed ripping its amorphous flesh with renewed zeal.

Neil and I took that as our cue to continue our own attacks and there was no time for further discussion on the possible use of the grenade.

While my pistol was now fully loaded, it still only carried six shots. I decided to holster it for the moment and switched my attention entirely to hacking away at the beast.

The drive of the shoggoth was impressive. I had seen my sword make shoggoths flee after only one cut, but this one was shrugging off the magical burns and slices, as well as wendigo attacks and bullets from an Esoteric Cavalry weapon.

That revelation made me fear what was contained within the scroll even more. If a contained Icthosthau could command one creature to wreak this kind of havoc with no value placed on its own survival, then what would he be like if he was released?

Limbs and chunks of flesh continued to fall as the shoggoth ignored us and slammed against the glass. I was close enough to hear the wards popping as he caused himself intense pain breaking them. Fractures throughout the glass grew wider and numerous enough that I couldn't make out the scroll behind it anymore.

Surprise struck me as a tentacle lashed out and wrapped around my sword and then my arm. The shoggoth's flesh was meant to devour everything that it touched, both body and soul, and I felt both fatigue and the intense burn akin to that of acid on my skin.

Twisting, I brought my blade and my arm down, slicing the

tentacle off and then flicking it away. My arm was covered with blisters and gaping holes that immediately began to fill with blood.

Much like the beast, I was driven as well and ignored the pain to continue my attack.

A blur of gray motion was the only indication that Carol had been thrown. I spared a quick glance when she landed and saw that her resilient wendigo flesh was mottled with burns and gaping holes. Her clawed hands looked as if they had been held in a fire and were covered in blisters. All of her fur between her hands and her elbows was missing.

Neil was suddenly swung around by his leg. His boot and pants would do little to protect him from the shoggoth's hungry touch. His screams confirmed this.

I stabbed it repeatedly, slamming my blade down as quickly as I could and creating new holes in the mass. It released Neil with a flick of its tentacle. Two new tentacles shot out and attempted to spear me. I spun and brought my blade down, avoiding one and cleaving the other from the main body.

The problem with human perception was that even the best of us could only pay attention to so much at a time, and while I was good, I certainly wasn't one of the best. A tentacle that I hadn't noticed grabbed my sword arm again, avoiding the sword this time. The searing pain began to sap my energy as the shoggoth feasted on my soul.

Dropping my sword, I snatched it with my other hand and sliced through the tentacle. It was now free from the body of the shoggoth, but unlike my previous strikes, it didn't let go. I could feel my life draining away from me as blood seeped out from under the slimy appendage.

If I didn't get rid of this thing, it wasn't going to just kill me, it would devour enough of my soul so that I wouldn't even get a chance to experience whatever the afterlife might hold for me. I would cease to exist, my allies would die, and Icthosthau would be free to reign over our world.

I swiftly brought my sword down on my arm, directly above where the tentacle was still feeding on me and just beneath my elbow. The blade of my sword was supernaturally sharp, and I was blessed with the sword going entirely through my arm on the first swing.

The blinding pain was so encompassing that I don't know what happened to the rest of my arm or the piece of the shoggoth that was still attached to it.

Unfortunately, I bought myself only a little time, as now I was likely to bleed out through my amputated arm. I could hear Nancy screaming behind me and for a moment I was relieved to hear her voice.

Then the words cut through the fog of my pain and filled me with terror.

"He's through the glass," she shouted.

I turned and saw what Nancy was describing. The shoggoth was taller than it had been and had mostly reverted to its Jack shape. Tentacles still shot out of it to slap Carol and Neil away, but he was using his human form to read the document.

The shoggoth spoke maybe ten words in the Hyperborean language and then dropped the scroll.

Laughter erupted from the shoggoth and it looked directly at me.

"You are too late. Icthosthau is here."

The scroll glowed with a throbbing yellow light that stretched to the ceiling. In the light, something was coming into existence.

"Screw this," Neil said as he threw the grenade.

I must have been losing too much blood, because I didn't even react as the grenade flew through the air.

A hand of black bone formed in the air and caught the grenade. The fingers of the hand were as long as my still-intact arm. The forearm that appeared was proportionately just as large. Swatches of dried flesh covered the black bones in patches. Laughter resonated throughout the room as the fist clenched around the grenade and pulled it closer to where I assumed the chest of Icthosthau was going to appear.

The explosion was muffled and the light from the scroll surged with the energy of it. Icthosthau used the grenade to blow open his tunnel to our world. Instead of the slow progress of appearing in front of us, he was suddenly just there.

He was a terrifying sight to see. His body was as tall as the ceiling of the armory and a terrifying mix of black bone and dried meat. His head was like nothing that I had seen before; it was made of more of that black bone and shaped like a mix of a deer and a tiger, but three times as large. His eyes were the fleshiest part of his body and were entirely red except for where white veins reached for his white irises.

As quickly as he appeared, he was suddenly replaced.

In Icthosthau's place stood a man covered in furs. He had a thick beard. Leather held the furs to his body, and he looked like a mountain man who had just returned to civilization. The only thing that remained of the monster that had briefly stood before us was his eyes.

Neil was still shooting, and Carol was on her knees in awe of this thing before her.

The edges of my vision were going dark. I was losing too much blood and realized that I was also on my knees. I hadn't even noticed that I'd fallen.

Icthosthau turned to the shoggoth and embraced it. As he did, the shoggoth finally started to show signs of pain. It writhed against Icthosthau's grip.

"Thank you," the demon spoke in a soft voice that was filled with emotion and gratitude. "Thank you for releasing me."

The shoggoth exploded. The armory was covered in shoggoth parts that began to melt, but none of it seemed to touch Icthosthau.

Icthosthau turned toward me and slowly walked over before kneeling next to me and touching the shoulder on my damaged arm.

"And thank you, Andrew," he looked around at the damage to the armory. "I'm sorry that your reward has been only destruction, but it was unavoidable." His eyes landed on Neil, who had stopped shooting and was just staring, then Carol, and then Nancy. "If you hadn't brought me fully into this world, I would not have been able to break my chains. I will destroy this world and enslave every being on it, but for you I offer this reward: your friends will survive. They will watch it all. I am a benevolent god."

From somewhere deep inside my dying body, I found some strength. "You came here to die." I spat blood at him as I spoke. "I will rip you from this universe and every universe. Your days are numbered in minutes."

Icthosthau smiled and bent lower to grab something just outside of my field of vision. He lifted it to where I could see. I watched with surprise as he held my sword by the blade in both hands and proceeded to snap it in half. The magic of the blade didn't even sizzle his skin.

"I doubt you'll have anything to do with it," he replied, and he slammed the broken blade into my neck. I felt it grind against my spine, and then I felt nothing.

Timothy

My eyes fluttered open and it took me a moment to get my bearings. I expected to still be in the armory, but that wasn't the case at all. I stood in the middle of a dirt street with shops and carts lining each side. The wares for sale were unlike anything you would find in a normal shop, and that was when I realized where I was.

The Dream Lands.

The last time that I had seen this street was when I had ditched Olivia in the Dream Lands. This street was normally a bustle of activity with people moving in such droves that you had to walk with the flow of them or risk getting swept away.

That wasn't the case now. The street was empty. The skies were dark. I was alone.

That was when a tearing sound brought my attention to a nearby stall and I recognized it almost immediately. When I had last been here, I had spoken with a being capable of containing my psychic parasite long enough for me to escape to my own body. This creature had lived under one of the stalls as a writhing mass of tentacles within a dark cloak. The tearing sound was coming from that same spot where he had been.

I walked over to the spot and crouched to see what was making the sound. There was a faint light in the darkness under the stall and I stepped forward to touch it.

As I reached for the light, my environment shifted, and I fell back into a sitting position.

The entire market street had changed into a large, empty void. Blackness and nothing stretched for as far as I could see.

Even beneath me seemed to be nothing, although I could feel a solid floor to stand on.

Directly in front of me was a large throne of a dark solid that was only visible because of its contrast with the nothingness. This throne was darker than the dark nothing that surrounded us and my mind warred with itself as it tried to comprehend the image. There was so much turmoil in my head that I almost didn't notice the being sitting on the chair.

"It's the chair, right? People always lose their minds over the chair." With a wave of something that was not a hand, I suddenly didn't care about the throne anymore.

Looking up, I took in the being before me.

"Hello, Timothy," I said.

"Hello, Andrew." His black robes obscured most of his body and all of his face, but I could hear the hint of a smile in his voice. "Do you know why you're here?"

I shook my head. "I figure that I must have died, but I expected more fire and brimstone, or at least the alien geometries of R'lyeh. I didn't expect a market vendor from downtown Dream Lands."

Timothy laughed at that and the sound had a psychic resonance attached to it. I felt his mirth. I enjoyed the sensation and in the back of my mind I wondered if that was the effect of his power or if I actually found comfort in this being.

"Don't tease me. You are smarter than that. Go ahead and take a guess."

"Your real name isn't Timothy," I replied. "You are one of the bastards playing at being a god. You are either going to make me a deal to save my life or you're about to start in on the eternity of torture for what I did to your people."

More mirth came at me from where the creature stood and this time, I joined in. My own laughter lacked the echo that his had, and I felt a flash of embarrassment that made no sense to me.

"There's that famous doctor I have heard so much about," he said. "I was beginning to wonder if you would live up to the hype."

Ignoring his commentary, I waved at him and added, "By

the form you've taken and your use of an Earthly language instead of just beaming your thoughts directly into my head, I am going to say that you are either Nyarlahotep or the Yellow King."

The tentacles, the robes, chair, and everything that made up this alien evaporated into a gas. A clapping started as an elderly man stepped out of the cloud of smoke.

"A human form, as well?" I added. "Nyarlathotep, then?"

"Impressive that you haven't started groveling yet." His body had changed but his voice still consisted of the booming resonance of his larger form. Nyarlathotep's amusement was finally evident on his face.

His radiating joy was no longer something that I could sense. It was replaced by my own feelings of terror. I shrugged, hiding my fear for what could come next behind false bravado.

"I've spent my entire life fighting the refuse from beyond the veil between worlds, and it's crossed my mind more than once that something somewhere wasn't going to just let me die." I crossed my arms. "Let's just say that I'm not surprised."

"Good," he spoke plainly but it resonated in my head as if he had shouted. "That makes everything easier. If you were a babbling and drooling mess on the floor, I probably wouldn't have much use for you."

"And what use does the god of chaos and madness have for me now?"

Nyarlathotep smiled and there was nothing that looked off about it, but I was filled with a sudden sense of dread.

"Perhaps I am working on behalf of one of the other gods? I've been known to aid them from time to time."

I shook my head. "Only when it suits you, I'm sure."

Nyarlathotep shrugged. "Your world is filled with monsters and champions, each with their own roles to play and their own miseries to live. There's something coming and it's going to be huge, and certain people need to remain in place to facilitate that event. Imagine going to the parlor and you can't get the big ice cream sundae because the guy in back is out sick. Well, I want all of the ice cream in the shop and I can't have it if anything goes off wrong."

"So, there's no deal?" I asked. "You need me alive, and I won't be allowed to die until your special chaos party is allowed to kick off?"

The god shook his head. "Nice try, but that's not the case at all. All of these monsters and champions are just greasing the wheel. I don't need any of them to make this happen, but if I want it to happen in the easiest way possible, they need to be in place." A small wooden chair appeared out of nowhere and Nyarlathotep sat down, crossing his legs. "A lot of things had to come together for me to make you this offer. Machinations that I put into place hundreds of years ago just so I would have this one option to send you back. If you go back and die again, that's it. I'll feast on your soul as we watch your world succumb to whatever it is that I am looking forward to."

Nyarlathotep's role in the universe was to inspire chaos, madness, and disaster. This coming crisis that he was alluding to was something that would give him more of what he craved, and by accepting any offer by him I would be subjecting my world to an upscale of what drove him. Chaos wasn't always bad, though. I needed more information.

"What is this event that's coming?" I demanded. "I can't make a decision uninformed."

"No," he said slowly, "that would be cheating. All you need to know is that if you are not there to usher it in, you cannot be there to try and stop it. The world can't be protected by the dead."

I noticed that he didn't say that it could be stopped, only that I couldn't try and stop it if I wasn't there. He was baiting the hook.

"Of course," he added, "I won't send you back at all if you don't agree to terms that I require."

Indecision was still consuming me. While I didn't have any reason to trust this thing that I saw as just another beast trying to meddle in the lives of Earth and its inhabitants, I didn't want to die, either. My life had been in the service of protecting humanity and I could accept a warrior's death, but I had family and friends that I selfishly didn't want to leave behind.

And Nancy.

I urged Nyarlathotep to continue.

"That's it," was all he said.

"What? What do you mean 'that's it?' You didn't say what your terms were." That sense of mistrust was only growing.

Nyarlathotep shrugged. "I am giving you back your life, which, as I understand it, is a huge deal to humans. So, the terms of this deal will become evident over time. I'll come to you at some point and make a request of either action or inaction and you will have no option but to agree to do as I ask. Failure to do so negates our deal." He spread his arms wide, "Until then, I'm letting you live under the good faith of our agreement."

He could ask me to do anything and I would be expected to do it. I could always refuse if the request was too large, and just die, removing any hold he would have over me.

The god was reading my mind. "That's the spirit. Start trying to figure out how you'll weasel out of this. I like it. You humans and your boundless hope are just the thing that keeps chaos spinning. It won't work, but struggle and squirm and justify this to yourself however you have to. At the end of the day, I have my proxy and you get to make kissy faces at your assistant. We all win." He stuck out his hand to me and asked, "Do we have an agreement?"

There was only one choice to make. There was no reason to believe that Nyarlathotep had told me the truth in anything that he had said. He might not even be reviving me, but the reality of the situation was dire. My team's numbers were down to three and they had to take on a demon wizard of nightmares from another world. None of them had any experience in that kind of thing, whereas I was getting a little bit more experience in it at this very moment.

I grasped Nyarlathotep's hand and shook. Immediately, a tendril of black energy lanced up my arm and toward my shoulder. As I followed it with my eyes I saw that a large piece of my shoulder was missing.

"I've been pulling the pieces of this deal together for centuries," he repeated. "Why else would I have an interest in a psychic emanation from your mind?"

It made sense, suddenly. In my hurry to get rid of Olivia

from my mind, I hadn't questioned Nyarlathotep's interest in her, assuming that he was interested in studying her odd existence. It had never occurred to me that in taking her he was leaving a small space in my mind and soul. A space that he could store something.

"What is that?" I screamed as the dark tendril found its place and filled the gap in my arm.

"You're my proxy now," Nyarlathotep spoke through a wide grin. "Consider this our ability to communicate. I've promoted you from a frail human to one of my frail avatars instead." He scrunched up his face like a doctor about to give a child a shot. "You won't even notice it's there."

As the dark energy merged with my spiritual flesh, it faded until it looked as if my shoulder was entirely whole and nothing had changed.

Nyarlathotep released my hand. "Our deal is sealed. Now I deliver on my promise so that you can someday deliver on yours."

The pain that followed was worse than anything I had ever experienced before.

Recovery

My lungs were on fire.

That was my first sensation after blacking out from my otherworldly meeting with Nyarlathotep. The pain was at an intensity unlike anything experienced in this plane of reality before. Or so I thought, before the feeling returned to the rest of my body. I was a map of every pain experienced by the human condition. I attempted to open my eyes and was greeted by the intense fire of the outside world. Focus eluded me and I found myself praying for death, the irony entirely lost on me in the moment.

After what seemed like an eternity of torture, the pain began to subside in waves. As the pain receded from my head, I realized that my eyes were open. Soon the blurry images resolved themselves into familiar shapes and I realized that I must be standing. My breathing was coming out shallow, but I didn't feel as though the pains from it were going to obliterate my soul, so I tried to speak.

"Where...?" was all that I managed to rasp out.

Suddenly, I could see clearly and the last of my screaming nerves quieted themselves. I was standing in my office, but everything was either knocked over or scattered to the floor. The only thing still on my desk was the Mi-Go brain jar with Jack's brain inside. Directly in front of me stood Carol. Her claws were out, and she was in a defensive stance. Behind her and to my left was Nancy with her machine gun out and on the opposite side was Sergeant Neil with his own pistol aimed in my direction.

"What happened?" I demanded.

Nancy slowly lowered her gun while the other two didn't

move. Before I knew it, she was hugging me and kissing all over my face. She was crying while she kissed me, and that seemed the strangest part of it. I hadn't seen Nancy cry since her father died.

While I appreciated the affection, I chose to break for air and repeat my question.

"You died" Carol answered, while shifting back into her human form.

The memories were still trying to surface through my residual pain. I remembered meeting with Nyarlathotep and the fact that I had died was an important part of that discussion. Then a new wave of pain flashed through my head and I remembered Icthosthau stabbing me in the neck with the broken blade of my magical sword.

"We know that you wouldn't have wanted us to revive you, especially," Carol waved toward the open military medical kit, "this way, but our options were limited and we can't stop Icthosthau without you."

I followed Carol's motions and stared at the kit. My mind still wasn't moving as quickly as I needed it to. Neil was saying something else, but I couldn't hear him over my sudden awareness of the medical kit. Something about it was nagging at my mind.

Absent-mindedly, I said, "Of course, I knew I had to come back, too."

Nancy asked what I meant, but I barely heard her.

The medical kit was open. Blood smeared its exterior. I assumed that it had to be my blood, but we had all sustained injuries in the last few hours. A roll of bandages was unraveled next to the case. Beside that was a large empty syringe. The syringe brought a sense of dread from somewhere deep in the back of my mind.

I looked down at my arms and my left arm was bandaged between my elbow and wrist. I flexed my fingers, and everything felt more or less normal, just a little bit different.

Then another memory flashed of me hacking off my own arm only moments before the shoggoth had managed to get the Scroll of Eibon. It was immediately followed by the memory of what had been in that syringe.

"You reanimated me?" I demanded. Then I held up my arm, "And why do I get the distinct feeling that this isn't my arm?"

Neil stepped forward and I noticed that sometime in the last few minutes he must have holstered his pistol. "We brought you to your office as soon as the demon thing left. Your arm had become mostly consumed by the shoggoth. Your secretary and assistant both said that while the Miksatonic Library might hold some information on how to fight Icthosthau, your slightly-more-traveled mind might contain information that was never committed to text." He sighed and cast a quick glance back at the two women. "While it was obvious that their opinions were clouded by their emotion, I couldn't deny that reviving you was the strategic choice."

I waved my hand at the mess that had previously been my office. "Then what happened?"

Worry furrowed the sergeant's brow as he continued. "We needed you whole, and the shoggoth had torn Ruddel to pieces. His arm was still intact, so we used the formula to revive you as well as reattach your arm. Almost instantly we watched as your wounds turned into scars and your arm fused to Ruddel's. Everything seemed to be going fine, until…"

"The sergeant said he's never seen anything like it," Nancy picked up. "You stood up and black clouds or energy or something poured out of you. Carol thinks it might have something to do with how much you've dabbled with magic not mixing well with the formula. When the energy vanished, you were in a rage and fighting each of us before you seemed to break from it."

Neil stepped in closer to me and held a finger up before I could respond. "Before you get all high and mighty about us reviving you, try to remember that I had to choose against reviving a member of my team on the slim chance that you could save us. Don't say one damn word about how we should have saved him or how we wasted the Lazarus serum. It wasn't your call to make."

I closed my mouth, knowing that he was right. I also had access to information that they didn't. Nyarlathotep had given me an option to return, and I hadn't even asked about Ruddel. He brought me back because I asked him to, knowing the consequences.

Nodding, I let it go and looked around some more.

Blood covered more than the medical bag. It also covered most of my desk and was smeared all over the floor. Looking to my friends, blood was covering them as well. I knew that it was mostly mine. If they had bled that much from the fight than they would have been just as dead as I had been.

"What happened to the cultists that were here?"

Nancy pointed in the general direction of the rest of the anthropology wing.

"We moved them to another room so that they weren't aware of what we were doing." She shrugged. "If they could mess it up, I'm sure they would. It was better that they didn't know."

"Thank you," I said. "The last thing I need is more credence to the rumors of my death." I changed the subject. "What happened to Icthosthau after I died?" It was a weird thing to say out loud.

Neil was the most prepared to answer that. "The 'prisoner god' paid us no attention and left the armory. Carol carried you up here and I did my best to block off the hall to the armory with some chairs and by ordering the staff to make signs. That's everything."

"Do you have any idea where Icthosthau might have disappeared to?"

Neil and Nancy shook their heads but also cast glances at Carol who had remained silent.

"Carol? Can you sense him?"

Her nod was almost imperceptible. She raised her arm and pointed toward my office window.

"I can still sense him," she answered, "stronger than when he was trapped in the scroll."

"Can you lead us to him?" I asked.

She nodded again. "I can take us to him, but I don't know how safe that will be. He's free and stronger now, it might be easier for him to control me." Carol let a tear travel down her cheek and added, "I cannot trust my own thoughts right now. He might want me to lead you right to him."

I reached out to her hand with my replaced arm, realized what I was doing, and switched hands. "You couldn't betray us, even if he were controlling you. What happened earlier wasn't on you."

Carol wiped her face, and it was like she had never shown any emotion. "It was, though. I should have fought harder."

"It wouldn't have done you any good," I countered. "This alien demi-god can manipulate our thoughts, and probably worse now that he's freed from his cage. If he hadn't pitted you against us, he still would have used Jack's shoggoth body against us."

"Can Itchy change reality?" Sergeant Neil was suddenly concerned again.

"Great question," I agreed.

Carol shrugged. "When he was in Hyperborea, his powers were described as endless. I don't believe that was the case, but he's already shown us that he can shape what we see and feel. It probably doesn't matter if he can change reality if he is capable of convincing us that he can."

"This isn't all bad," I forced a smile. "We can find..." I pointed at Neil, "Itchy and we know what he can do. Now we just need to figure out how to kill him or put him back into the scroll."

"That's an awfully big piece of the puzzle," Neil said.

I shrugged at him. "I've traveled across the world to enter an alien city with nothing but a madman, a Frenchie, and the madman's daughter and that turned out alright. This time we at least know what we're fighting and where it came from."

"Either way," Nancy cut in, "Itchy might not be the current priority."

"Why is that?" I asked.

Neil answered for her. "There are monsters all over the city. Obviously, the majority of them are figments from people's nightmares brought to life, but a few of them are real and attracted to working with the demon."

I shook my head. "Itchy is still the priority. Most of those monsters will disappear when we put him down."

Carol turned to the sergeant and said, "Let us leave them some time to figure out the next steps. I think you and I should do a perimeter check and maybe check on our guests in the next room."

As they left, I took a moment and examined my new arm just a little closer. The scar where the two halves of arm met was still red as if it were still at the end of a long healing cycle. It was thick, too, and created a clear divide between the two limbs. Rolling my new arm over I found a tattoo on the inner wrist. It was a cross with a date inside of it.

2-20-27.

I had no idea who it was remembering, but I couldn't help but want to fulfill whatever promise Ruddel had made them.

I called out to Neil as he picked up Jack's jar. "Before I go out there, I need to know what side effects there are with the serum."

"None in the newest formula," he answered immediately.

"Yet," the voice of Jack crackled over hidden speakers on the jar. It startled me. I knew that he would be able to talk, but the last time I had seen that jar, I had switched it off.

"Hello, uh, Jack. It's a pleasure to finally meet the real you." I stuttered out.

"What's left of me, anyway," the speaker let out an audible sigh before adding, "A pleasure to meet you as well, Dr. Doran."

"What do you mean by 'yet?'" I asked the brain and former medic.

Jack's voice was more timid than it had been as mimicked by the shoggoth. "No formula has been perfected and this formula hasn't been field tested enough for conclusive results. No formula has ever managed to get rid of the 5% chance of complete mental breakdown." He paused before continuing, "Your unique relationship with … things means that you will probably discover any possible side effects sooner rather than later."

"Great," I sighed.

Neil either didn't hear the sarcasm dripping in my voice or chose to ignore it. "It can be," he explained. "In all cases, there is increased longevity."

"He'll live longer?" Nancy's voice perked up. "How much?"

Jack's speaker, wherever it was hidden on the jar, crackled as he answered. "All subjects that haven't been terminated, whether they are insane or not, are still currently alive. In 1917, the formula was administered to an 82-year-old woman on her deathbed and she is still alive and physically healthy today."

"Physically?" I asked. "So, her mind is a complete wreck?"

Neil didn't answer with words, but his facial expression was answer enough.

The heavy silence was shattered when I clapped my hands together.

"That is entirely tomorrow's problem." I looked from Nancy to Carol and then to Neil. "Would you all be willing to give me a moment alone with Nancy, please?"

Carol and the sergeant nodded and walked out of the office, carrying Jack's jar.

"You were kissing me," I pointed out as soon as the door was shut.

Nancy's cheeks flushed and the corners of her mouth formed into a tight grin. "Of course I was," she said. "I was happy that you weren't dead anymore."

I allowed myself to relax, if only for a minute. No one was trying to kill us, I wasn't dead anymore, and the world hadn't ended yet. I returned her grin.

"We are going to have to sit down and figure us out," I said.

Nancy leaned in and softly touched my cheek. "I can't imagine that there's much to talk about."

Her hand was soft, but it reminded me of the things I was allowing myself to forget. I pulled away from her touch.

"At any moment, I could go insane and kill you," I pointed out. "I am a bomb just waiting to go off, now. And that's only the side-effect that we can predict. My connection to the veil could be the trigger that creates the worst combination of things to come about with this formula."

"You mean the man with the black eyes?" Nancy's voice was still soft but there was a hardness in it that wasn't there before.

I nodded, "That's just one example, but yes. I'm just not safe to be around and you're thinking about something more than that."

Nancy's face went red with rage. "You obnoxious idiot. That was the problem before you could turn feral." She walked to the chair that her gun was leaning against and picked it up. "You had no problem dragging me to an alien city filled with Nazis and proto-shoggoths or to an ancient cave that leads to another planet in another dimension or telling me to shoot at monsters straight from our nightmares, but getting close to you is 'too dangerous'?"

She chambered the magazine before adding, "You're either stupid or not interested. If you're not interested, then say so and I can get back to work."

My mind reeled at the very obvious point she made. I was an idiot. After what seemed like forever, my brain finally kicked itself back into gear.

"I am definitely interested."

She smirked as she said, "So, you're just stupid then?"

I shrugged. "I just don't want to hurt you."

"Then you shouldn't have invited me to Antarctica," she repeated. "You did, though, and I'm here. The odds are that we're going to die today, and you're right, you might go insane, but I would rather face that smiling and knowing where we stand."

"Maybe I'm going crazy," I said, "because that makes sense. So, where do we stand?"

Nancy grabbed me by the collar and pulled me in for a deep kiss. If it weren't for her tommy gun we would have probably wrecked my office, but the metal reminded both of us that we still had a job to do.

When we broke, Nancy slung the strap of her gun over her shoulder. "We're going to lock Icthosthau back up and then you're going to take me to dinner. No seafood." She stepped back up to me and gave me another, shorter, kiss. "Now stop feeling sorry for yourself and get out there. The Esoteric Cavalry needs Dr. Doran's help."

I smirked. "That's one of the neatest parts of all this."

Nancy returned my smile. "The army needs our help? Yes, that's crazy."

My assistant turned and headed toward the door but

stopped when she saw that I hadn't gotten back up yet.

"Are you coming?"

"In a minute," I answered. "Can you send Carol in first?"

"You're not going to kiss her, too, are you?" Nancy laughed.

Frowning, I replied, "Not on purpose."

Nancy left with a bounce in her step and soon Carol replaced her.

My secretary sniffed the air before saying, "Thank the gods that finally happened."

"Finally?" I asked.

"You don't live as long as I have without noticing things."

My mood turned grim. "It sounds like that could be me."

"You don't have to ask," Carol's voice was cold and very professional. "I'll do it."

"No hesitation?" I had to know that it would be done.

Her calm demeanor broke as anger or hurt lanced across her expression. "I said I would do it, don't ask me to be a monster. Not even for you." She recomposed herself. "I've worked for many Deans, and you are by far the worst—"

"Thank you," I interrupted.

Carol continued. "You're also one of the very few to not treat me as less than human. You're the first I have ever considered a friend. For that reason, if you lose your mind or become unstable I will kill you, but I cannot promise that I won't hesitate."

"That is all that I can ask for. Thank you." I shifted the subject. "How are you feeling?"

"Much better," she answered. "I no longer feel the call of the scroll. I think that Icthosthau sent out the call in order to release himself, and no longer has a need for me."

"That is what I had been hoping," I said. With Icthosthau out of the scroll, he didn't need to beg every monster in Arkham to come to his aid and the madness he was putting into Carol had subsided.

Carol continued, "Unfortunately, sir, I don't think that I can be trusted to fight him."

"Why?" I couldn't hide the concern in my voice.

Carol's professional veneer cracked as she explained. "I can feel him everywhere all at once." She tapped the back of her head and squinted. "It's like an itch in the back of my mind that can only be relieved if I let myself revert to my natural state. While his powers aren't forcing me to turn, I feel that he could exercise control over me if I were to get too close to him."

While annoyed that our own best weapon against Itchy was now benched, I couldn't help but be relieved that she had told me this when she did.

"I would rather you stay out of this fight and keep safe, than have you out there and hurting those you love," I told her.

Carol rarely smiled, but she let one through in that moment. "Don't get ahead of yourself, sir. I told you that I considered you a friend, not that I loved you."

"Very funny." I turned to the window. "Stay close to campus, then. Keep the students and faculty safe. If you feel yourself losing control, come and lock yourself in here. The wards should keep you locked in until I come and get you."

"Or course," she agreed. "You will make me the same promise?"

We hugged and I told her that I would. "One way or another, we won't become monsters. I promise."

No sooner had our hug broken when the very door I said would keep a wendigo locked safely away from the public exploded inward, toward us.

Through the debris walked a woman who wore the shadows like a cloak.

While I was still flinching, Carol was a blur of speed and leaped at this new attacker. A shadow broke from the cloaked woman and grabbed Carol like a tentacle, slamming her against my bookshelves and pinning her there.

Instinctively I reached behind the veil of reality to the power between worlds, and prepared myself to throw a blast of my own magic.

Instead, a crippling pain shot through my temples and the sensation of fire filled my veins. I fell to my knees, screaming with the pain.

Behind my own screams of pain, I could hear the shadow witch laughing. "The great Andrew Doran not only died, but has been resurrected like some Biblical figure." She was in front of me, caressing my face as I struggled to push away the still-searing pain. "Do they know how they have ruined you?" She didn't expect me to answer. "Do not worry, hero. I am here to undo their mistake." A shadow lanced out behind her and into the bookshelves near where Carol was pinned. A scream from the next room over told me that she had just killed our Traum Kult captives and informed me who had sent the witch.

Through gritted teeth, I asked, "Why did you kill your own people?"

"They were loose threads that needed to be cut."

The shadow blades arced in toward me as they prepared to remove my head from my shoulders.

My body was still racked by pain, but I managed to bring my arm up and put my pistol beneath her chin. As the bullet passed through her head, the shadows fell apart and seemed to slither to their homes under tables and behind chairs.

When Carol fell to the floor, I heard her say, "That was odd."

I agreed. "I think we just witnessed the first side-effect of my resurrection. The serum, or my new state of being, seem to block my access to the magic beyond the veil."

"That as well," she said, "but I was referring to the sudden and brazen attack."

"More of the Traum Kult, or whatever they are calling themselves now, are going to be taking advantage of the distraction Icthosthau is providing. There's never been a better time to make a move on the campus."

"Why come here at all, though?" she asked. "Originally, they were making their attacks in an attempt to get their hands on the Scroll of Eibon, but the scroll has been used and they shouldn't have any motivation behind another assault."

I pointed in the direction of where Neil and Nancy had stored our captives. "To silence them, I suppose. Without them, we have no idea who else on campus might be working with them."

Carol's eyes lit up. "Or they were never here for the scroll in the first place."

Sighing, I tried getting back on my feet.

Pain surged through my body and I threw up.

Getting Back Up

Getting back to my feet was a battle of unearthly proportions. Every movement had to be slowly planned in advance. First, I straightened my feet and planted them on the floor. Then I gathered my strength and pushed myself skyward.

My nerves sang as if electricity was surging through them from the base of my feet and all the way to my hair. I didn't remember actually standing, but had somehow managed through the pain. Grabbing a nearby chair, I almost fell down again as another wave of nausea hit me.

When I had run out of stomach contents to dump on my office floor, I realized that I was starting to feel better. I had no doubts that this was a lingering side-effect of my return to the land of the living. I hoped that this wasn't some negative reaction by my body to the normal food that was in my stomach. I wasn't mentally ready to start eating the living yet.

I nodded in response to the raised eyebrow that I was receiving from Carol. I was as ready as I was ever going to be, and any more time wasted meant more people were likely to die.

My secretary tilted her head to the side as something outside of my normal human hearing caught her attention.

"The battle with the cultists is far from over," she said.

A thought suddenly occurred to me. "Didn't Neil and Nancy just leave the room?"

Carol nodded.

"The shadow witch would have had to go by them to get to us." I ran at the hole that was once my office door, stopping only to scoop up my pistol. I cast a quick glance at my scabbard, with the hilt to my magical sword sticking out of it. One of my last pre-death memories was of that blade being broken. I would have to lament the loss later.

We were down the hall and had managed to catch up to Nancy and Neil in seconds. They were fighting two more of what I assumed to be cultists. They were dressed like students and weren't carrying any weapons but had managed to disarm both Nancy and the well-trained military combatant.

As fast as I was under normal circumstances, I would never reach wendigo levels of speed. It didn't help me at all that I was slowed by my still recovering from being dead.

Carol bounded over me like a human-shaped lion and collided with both of the cultists attacking our friends. It was over in the blink of an eye as both of the former students exploded into shredded strips of meat.

Nancy held up her arms. "Why are they still attacking us?" She waved about to indicate the current state of the world. "Can't they tell that the scroll has already been used up?"

"We don't think that they were ever here for the scroll," I explained.

"Then what are they here for?" The sergeant panted as he asked.

I shook my head. "We don't know." I pointed at the still-warm parts sprayed all over the hall, "This is a lot of people hitting us when things are starting to really spin out of control. It feels like they are trying to take advantage of the situation."

"And it looks like the campus and much of Arkham are affected by the nightmares." Neil was finally getting his breath under control. Straightening up, he added, "Why aren't they?"

I frowned. Cultists were taking over the school while it was being overrun by nightmare projections from an otherworldly demon-god. "Are we certain that they aren't also nightmares?"

"Oh," Nancy caught on to my train of thought, "as if your nightmare would be losing the school to endless horror and enemy cultists?"

I nodded. "Exactly."

Carol shook her head. "I can smell them." She licked her lips. "I can taste them. They are more real than the projections."

"Damn," I cursed. It would have been nice to know we were still only dealing with a single enemy. Instead we would be fighting this battle on two fronts, and no war could do that for too long. "We've got what feels like the entirety of the Traum Kult here while an alien demon summons our worst nightmares to torment our campus and town. I don't know what to do."

It was a solid ten seconds of silence before I realized my other fear. I flexed my new arm, Tim's arm, and wondered if the tingling sensation that ran down it was another product of my resurrection or my imagination. The majority of my nausea and sluggishness was beginning to pass and I felt mostly normal again, but the nagging fear at the back of my mind wouldn't go away.

How was I supposed to fight Icthosthau and the revived Traum Kult without the power from the veil or my magical sword?

The sword was only the newest tool in my arsenal and I would learn to adapt to not using that, but the magic hit me a little closer to home. I had spent years using magic to supplement my strategies. Magic had shifted in my life from an essential tool to the only tool that I used to keep the monsters at bay. So much so that it had caused my personality to split and birthed the psychic emanation that was Olivia.

My rebirth via the Green Lazarus took that all away from me. Having seen previous versions of the serum in action, I figured I would be able to resist more physical force than before I had died, and I would have the added benefit of a longer life, but what was any of that if I was helpless to protect the people, city, and country that I cared about?

I was beginning to drift down a dark mental path and had to shake myself out of it.

"We need a plan," I said.

Nancy shook her head. "No, we don't. There's only one plan."

Everyone was quiet so I asked, "And … that would be?"

Nancy frowned at us. "You're all incredibly disappointing right now." Sighing, she explained. "We can't figure out who is or isn't a cultist since they look like students and it does us no good to fight the projections." She pointed at Carol. "She can lead us to Itchy. Taking him out will stop the projections and free us up to sort out the students. So, for now, we take the fight to Itchy."

Nancy's explanation left no doubt that she was right. We were all incredibly disappointing.

"She's right," Neil said before I could. "Cut off the head and then we can worry about the lesser threat when we have the time.

"Carol," I turned to see the administrative assistant licking her fingers. I paused to let her stop. She looked sheepish but didn't apologize. "Can you sense how far away Icthosthau is?"

She wiped the rest of the gore off on parts of the victim's clothing that were still dry before she answered. "I thought that the plan was for me to stay back in your office so that I didn't hurt anyone?"

"That was when my office had a door," I explained. "If you can handle it, I would like to keep you with me for as long as possible."

Carol nodded in agreement before answering my question, "I can sense which direction to go and I can tell you that he is still on the campus. Unfortunately, that's about it. I won't know more until we are closer to him and that would be … dangerous."

At Nancy and the sergeant's concerned looks, I explained, "She's worried that the closer she gets to Itchy, the more likely it will be that he will be able to control her again."

"Well," Nancy smiled, "we still need you. We will just have to trust you to let us know when we're on our own."

"Until then," Neil said, "we can't afford to split up anymore."

Agreeing, I added, "That means we can't go out of our way to save students, faculty, or anyone." I saw in Nancy's eyes that she didn't like that idea, and added, "The longer we take to save a handful of people fighting Icthosthau's monsters out there, the more people are going to die. We have to stop him and stop all of this at once."

Their solemn silence was all I received as acknowledgement. We reloaded our guns and checked ourselves over one last time. The halls seemed emptier than ever before, and we were comfortable knowing that Carol would hear any sort of cultist attack while we prepared ourselves. It was our last quiet moment of peace before we stepped out onto the campus.

When everyone was ready, I stepped forward and opened the same doors that Jack had held shut during the onslaught of the imaginary undead invasion.

We stepped out into a warzone.

The Warzone

The grass burned in patches.

Every type of monster was attacking every student or faculty member. In many of the cases it looked as if terrifying them was the goal but there were instances spread out all over the quad where terrorizing a student meant drawing blood or maiming them.

To my surprise, I can even recognize some of the Traum Kult's people simply by the nightmares chasing them. The odds of a shoggoth being the nightmare of a freshman were highly unlikely and I tried to make a mental note of them.

"Where do we even start?" Nancy asked.

"With Icthosthau," the Sergeant answered.

I nodded, "He's right. The longer we ignore the real problem, the more people will die."

"We can't ignore them," Nancy's terror was starting to question her resolve.

I stepped forward and grabbed at the nearest nightmare. It was a large man who was balding and smelled of alcohol but he had muscles on top of muscles that made him look ridiculous. He was stalking after a kid in a leather jacket and chanting "Never good enough," through clenched teeth.

He spun at my touch and swung at me. I ducked under the swing and drew my pistol. I fired once into his head and he didn't seem to notice. That only confirmed what we already knew from the previous nightmares; they couldn't be killed but could otherwise be slowed down. My second bullet tore through his knee and he went down with a groan. The kid in the leather jacket turned and ran without saying anything.

"We won't ignore the ones directly in our path," I answered Nancy. "That doesn't change our mission."

Carol started walking through the battlefield and the rest of us fell in line behind her. I put myself close to Nancy. She didn't need my protection and I had every faith that she could fight as well as anyone else in our group, but her pale expression told me she needed a presence near her for emotional strength.

The things that people feared ranged from understandable fears to the ridiculous. Near the central fountain I saw two of the faculty wrestling with a Nazi soldier who was still wearing a parachute while just a few feet away from them, a cartoon cat with an oversized head was trying to drown the janitor assigned to the music wing.

Neil shot the cat, giving the janitor a chance to stand up and run.

Suddenly, Nancy was standing in front of me. It was so sudden that I walked into her. Instead of her bouncing back as we collided, she pushed me to the ground. As I fell, I crashed into another Nancy and realized something was wrong.

"He would still be alive if it wasn't for you," the nightmare Nancy shouted at me. She lifted me off the ground with one hand and placed a pistol beneath my chin. I hadn't seen the pistol, but I had no doubt that it was the same gun that Olivia had used to kill Nancy's father.

The real Nancy grabbed at her double and tried to pry her hand off of me. I heard the click of the hammer as Nancy's eyes bore into me.

"Why do you do it?" the nightmare demanded. "You know that everyone you drag along with you is going to die," she let out a giggle that up until that moment had always made me smile when I heard it from the real Nancy's lips. "Or worse. How many people have you turned into monsters? How many widows and orphans have you left in your wake?"

"Don't listen to her," the real Nancy Dyer shouted as she and Neil struggled to pull me out of the nightmare's grip. "It's just Olivia messing with you."

"No, it's not," I said. My nightmare of this scenario was never of Olivia trying to use Nancy to torture me. The eyes looking up at me with all of that rage were Nancy's.

"You didn't even hesitate to replace your last victim with me," the monster said. "Was Leo even cold before you offered me his job?"

A blur of gray slammed into nightmare Nancy and I fell to the ground. Carol grappled with her for only a second before throwing her almost a hundred yards with her wendigo strength.

I stood up and Nancy was looking me over and asking me if I was alright.

"Yes," I could tell my smirk was confusing my companions, "she just told me something that can help us."

"What did she tell you?" Neil demanded.

Looking around us, I decided that we needed to get somewhere safer before I took the time to explain. "Carol, where are we headed?"

She pointed to the building at the end of the quad. "It looks like Icthosthau might be consolidating his power in the campus museum."

"I'll explain when we're safer." The ground began to shake as I stood up. "This one isn't one of mine," I said.

The sergeant's face turned white. "No," he gasped. "Not this."

"Not what?" I demanded.

"Run." His voice was a whisper, but it was all we needed to motivate us faster toward the museum.

Behind us, the ground erupted. Dirt and stone flew across the campus and rained down on us.

A worm or snake, the size of a bus and with a mouth of tooth-covered tentacles was darting around looking for something to eat. Most of the faculty and students had managed to avoid the thing's reach but one student wasn't so lucky. A piece of debris from the worm-thing's arrival had hit her leg and she went down. That was all it had needed to scoop her up. As the serrated tentacles tossed her toward the gaping maw, they also shredded her. By the time she entered the creature she was already dead, and in a thousand pieces.

We burst through the door of the museum and slammed

it shut behind us. Carol pulled a key from seemingly nowhere and locked the door behind us. We stood in the lobby of the museum. It was a small room that consisted of a standard desk and doors at the back and to the sides to explore the various wings. Miskatonic University's museum was an understated collection of impressive historical artifacts. I had helped prepare and curate a small number of the items on display and could vouch for the fact that the university preferred to put all of its efforts behind understanding and researching an item and almost nothing behind how fancy the building was that we put them in.

"What was that thing?" Nancy was panting.

"An uverdengrope," Neil replied, on his knees as he rested. "I saw one eat an entire village in North Dakota while my men tried to evacuate it. They eat and they don't die."

Uverdengrope were a new one to me, but I wasn't surprised. The United States Esoteric Cavalry had been around longer than I had been alive, so it was likely that they had seen some things that I hadn't yet.

Hopefully, I would never have to see that thing again.

"Are we safe in here?" I asked.

Neil shook his head, "Nowhere is safe from the real one. I can only imagine that the nightmare version is worse."

"Wonderful." Nancy rolled her eyes and turned to take in our surroundings. "I can't say I have been in here before," she addressed Carol. "Do you know where Itchy will be hiding?"

Carol didn't answer right away so I went ahead with my admonishment. "You work for the Dean, whose doctorate is in Archaeology, of the most prestigious school for studying occult history, and you've never been to the University Museum before?"

Nancy smirked, "Should I have done that before or after I was helping Carol cover for your complete lack of work ethic, Dean?"

Before I could address this sudden employee insubordination, I noticed that Carol was shaking.

"I shouldn't be here," she said in a whisper.

Her skin had turned a shade whiter and her eyes had sunken

a little further into her skull, but she seemed to be keeping her human shape. That was my only real gauge for how close to losing control Carol was. She held onto her humanity not just in mindset but also in physical form. If she totally lost it, we would know before she attacked only because she would want to sink her incredibly large wendigo fangs into our necks.

"What will happen if we go further?" I ask her.

Carol shook her head. "If I get any closer, you won't be able to trust me."

"Can you stay here?" I indicated the lobby.

Carol nodded, but it didn't seem to have much confidence.

"Good," I showed her a smile to provide her with the confidence that I wasn't feeling. "We're going to need you to keep a mountain-sized uverdengrope from attacking us from behind."

Carol returned my smile. "Shouldn't be much harder than convincing an entire college that their dean is hard at work on the new budget."

I pointed a finger at her and then Nancy, "I never wanted the job, so get off my back." Then I aimed that same finger at the double doors at the other end of the room, "Can we get back to the plan of attacking the alien god?"

As soon as my finger pointed at the doors, they burst open and the museum director, Edmund Taylor, came running at us.

"Dr. Taylor," I greeted him, but it was obvious from his look that he wasn't here to give us a tour.

"If you brought guns," he called as he sprinted toward us, "I suggest you prepare to use them."

Looking to where he had come from, we saw a group of flesh beasts like I had never seen before come squeezing through the doors. They were at least twice as large as the doors and they seemed to be shaped from a mix of different body parts. In some instances, it looked like entire bodies had been merged together into these creatures of muscle and mass. None of the three that first came through the doors looked the same.

None of us hesitated and we opened fire. They were more monsters from Icthosthau's nightmare powers, and I was sure of it because my gun was faring no better than anyone else's.

When the first two fell, two more replaced them, pushing their way through the smaller door frame.

I couldn't help but be reminded of my new failings. The flesh monsters tore through the front desk as they came toward us, and I had to stop myself from reaching for the powers behind the veil. On one instance instinct almost overcame me, and I felt the burning pain surge through my blood when I began to collect the power for a spell.

Clutching my chest, I fell to my knees briefly and quickly began reloading my pistol to hide my failure.

"We need to block the door," Neil shouted over the gunfire. Carol switched to that task as we each chose a nightmare flesh-beast and focused on it. As our monsters each fell, Carol shoved the remains of the front desk and one of the large display cases in front of the door.

"How are you going to move forward and fight Icthosthau when we can't even go past the lobby?" Carol asked.

Edmund was talking to the sergeant, and it was easy to see that Neil was working on an answer to Carol's question already.

Nancy walked up to me and softly touched my arm. "I saw you fall." Concern filled her expression. "Are you alright?"

How do you tell the person you are beginning to connect with how weak you feel without your extra-human abilities that they never had to begin with? How do you tell them that you feel useless when you are as limited as they are?

You just do.

"I have been using magic for so long," I said. My eyes fell to the arm that was now mine. "This gift you have all given me has had a side-effect. My new life can't use magic anymore."

She seemed to understand, and she squeezed my arm. "You're more than the magic."

Neil broke from Edmund and turned toward me.

"Don't be an ass, Doran," he jabbed me in the chest. "The Esoteric Cavalry didn't come to you for your ability to throw spells like some militant Merlin. We would have taken the scroll from you, and more, the minute we could if we thought that was all you were. We let you keep your armory and your," he scoffed, "mission because you're an expert of ancient evils. You know more about this shit than anyone." He jabbed me again. "So quit trying to cheat your way out of these situations and start thinking your way out."

He was right. The magic had come to me as I traveled the world and expanded my education. Every experience I shared with a native islander or a Ulthar priestess taught me more about the world and the mechanics behind it. My education, both during and after school had given me the spells that I had been leaning on so heavily, but they had also given me so much more. I knew how the world of the occult worked and needed only to tap into that knowledge in a more traditional way if I was going to survive long enough to confront Icthosthau.

The edge of an idea began to surface in my mind. My eyes cast about the lobby and the shattered shelves as I looked for what we had at our disposal that could assist us with these beasts or perhaps much more.

Miskatonic University's museum wasn't an homage to the esoteric of the world. Most of the world, even on this campus, didn't acknowledge anything outside of their world views, even if it was directly in front of them. Things from the ancient past were mixed together because that was how history really was. The occult didn't exist separate from the rest of history. It was mixed in and part of history. When your average student of archaeology or history professor would study anything, they would present it through the filter of their own world view.

If you showed that history professor a shadow banishment rod of the Night Watchers, they would attribute it as a ritual pipe of the Mayans. They wouldn't be wrong, but they wouldn't be anywhere close to correct.

My attention fell on a small bowl with markers from an Iroquois collection that we kept near the front. So many of those bowls had been donated to the museum that everyone assumed they were simply bowls, but I knew better. They each had a small set of symbols that, when interpreted, spoke to mental clarity.

More specifically, the filtering of bad dreams.

"I have an idea," I shouted as I scooped up the bowl.

"About time," Neil said.

"I need blood," I said. "Fresh blood."

We weren't short on injuries. The sergeant's wounds were more grievous, though. He proffered his arm and I had to press on his wound to get enough blood collected into the bowl. To his credit, he didn't make a sound at the damage I caused him.

"A lighter, as well?" Edmund tossed me his Zippo and I lit several of the brochures that had spilled across the floor, allowing the ashes to fall into the bowl.

I went to Nancy first.

I dipped my finger into the mixture of ash and blood and drew on her forehead. The symbol itself didn't matter nearly as much as the importance of the symbol and its meaning to me. I drew the first sign of protection that I had ever learned in my esoteric studies. It was a crude star with an eye in the middle. The Elder Sign.

"What does this do?" Nancy asked me.

"Native cultures all have means of protecting themselves from dreams," I explained. "They understand that the world of dreams isn't just a fictional realm in our minds, but an entire reality that can press into our own." I held up the bowl. "This should filter the influence of the nightmares coming at us." I didn't mention that it would also help me prove a theory I was desperate to know the status of.

Dr. Taylor seemed to have an epiphany. "Are these creatures from the Dream Lands?"

I was impressed, but not surprised, by his knowledge of the Dream Lands.

"We think so," I answered, "but we aren't sure. These could be psychic impressions or spiritual creations. If this works, then we can narrow it down and perhaps fight the influence with more effect."

"That explains the fleshadons," he said.

"Fleshadons?" Nancy asked. "Those things just now?"

Edmund nodded. "I have never seen one before. They were only something I had read about."

"Well, that put them into your mind and our current situation put them into our world," I agreed.

"How do we test it?" Carol asked.

I shrugged. "Open the door, I guess."

She rolled her eyes. "Great idea. Why didn't I think of that?"

My secretary and the sergeant pulled the blockade away from the right side of the double doors. Carol pressed herself against the door to be the supernatural strength that held the door in place as they slowly opened it.

From where I stood, I couldn't see the flesh-beasts behind the door. It was obvious that they were there, though, as they slammed into the door in an attempt to get past Carol and at us.

Nancy stepped forward and peeked around the edge of the door before immediately leaping back and bringing up her gun.

"I can still see them," she shouted, and then fired through the gap. "Am I supposed to still see them?"

"Probably not," I shouted back as I leapt forward to help Carol shut the door.

The ash and blood spell of the Iroquois should have worked. At least, it should have if my theory about how Icthosthau worked had been correct. Unfortunately, I had missed something.

That was when I saw Carol's forearm bleeding and had an idea.

Using my sleeve, I wiped the bowl as clean as I could and started over.

"We need Hyperborean blood," I said to Carol as I grabbed her arm. She growled at me and I flinched, remembering who, exactly, I had grabbed and added, "Can I borrow some blood?"

"I don't think I'll want it back," she said through half a snarl.

Again, I ran through the mechanics of the spell. Squeezing some of her blood and burning whatever paper I could find into the bowl. Once it was complete, I returned to Nancy.

"Ready to try again?" I asked.

She frowned at my question. "Do I have a choice?"

I nodded to Carol and she began opening the door. Again, I was positioned behind Carol to assist her if the door became too much. My only indications that the creatures were still behind the door were the sudden slamming against my secretary and myself and the gasp from Edmund as the door slipped further than Carol or I intended.

Nancy stepped forward and looked from the door to past it

and then back to the door before looking at me.

"I can still see them," she said, "but they are like ghosts." She stepped toward the doorway and I started, holding out my hand. Nancy waved me off. "I need to see if they can still touch me."

Of course, she was right. It made me uncomfortable and I regretted letting her be the first person to test the spell and briefly wondered if the madness from my resurrection was already affecting me.

Nancy approached the door cautiously before jumping through the gap that was provided. I couldn't help myself and let go to run around and watch what happened.

She was buffeted by winds, or at least that is what it looked like. I could still see the flesh-beasts as they swung at her and tried to tear her limb from limb. Each swipe at her face was nothing more than a gentle push that she had to lean into. Before the monsters could give up and turn their attention to me, Nancy was back through the door and we were barricading it again.

"So," Neil asked, "it worked?"

Nancy nodded, "It worked. I could see them, but they couldn't affect me."

"It won't last forever, though," I added. "The spell only lasts for as long as the blood is still wet."

"That's hardly useful," Neil said. "Blood dries quickly."

I shook my head, "Normally, yes, but we're dealing with Hyperborean blood. It is magically charged. We might get half an hour out of it."

"That's still not that long," Edmund said.

I turned toward our newest arrival and started drawing the same Elder Sign on his forehead. "We don't have enough guns, Ed, or I would ask you to come with us. Do you have some place that you can go to hide?"

"What about the students?" he asked.

"Students?" I looked around, trying to see what he could be referencing.

"There was a contingent of faculty and students on a tour of the facility. They..." he looked confused as he sought the correct word, "seemed to go mad."

"Wonderful," Nancy sighed behind me.

"We'll look out for them," Neil said, "but stopping the demon thing is our priority. If we can stop him, they should go back to normal."

I could tell that he wasn't entirely sure about that, so I nodded to give him what I hoped was confidence.

Not that I believed it. Hope was our last refuge.

Edmund said that he had a place he could get to and took off to the left side of the lobby where a small door led to either a stairwell or a janitor's closet. Either way, I had to hope that he would remain safe.

Nancy drew the Elder Sign on me and together we finished drawing it on the sergeant and Carol. Even though Carol still didn't plan on coming with us, I wanted her to feel whatever relief she could from the pressure of her "prisoner god."

Thanking her, I nodded toward the door that Edmund had hidden behind.

Carol returned my nod, "I will keep him safe and stop any attacks from behind you."

I pocketed the small ceremonial bowl and asked Carol for one more, rather large, favor.

I gave her Leo's flask, that I had almost forgotten was on me, and she dripped more of her blood in there. When she gave it back it felt like it was close to half full. She tied off the wound and took up a position in the center of the room.

Neil shook her hand in thanks and Nancy pulled Carol into a big hug before we went to work pulling down the barricade in front of the double doors.

Again, we only removed the barricade from one of the doors, allowing us to control the flow of monsters that might come bursting through. To our surprise, there was no noise on the other side of the door.

We inched it open to see the monsters were no longer there.

"Perhaps Itchy decided to give up when his projections weren't working," Neil suggested.

"That would be great if I believed it for even a second," I mumbled.

We turned down the hall and toward the Egyptian wing.

Miskatonic Museum

A ny other museum would have the halls lined with displays and posters about upcoming events and touring exhibits. The university's museum wasn't the standard by any means. Its goal was to house the artifacts collected by the many sanctioned digs and excursions by the school's team of archaeologists, art students, and geologists. While we didn't discourage anyone and everyone from visiting the collection, we put them on display for students to study them, for research projects to be focused on, and as a place to display the efforts of our excursions for those who gave us the money to conduct them.

Everybody liked seeing their name above a wing in the campus museum.

For that reason, the Egyptian wing was called, this month, the Carter Hall.

Even without the fanfare of decorations, the hall was impressive. Miskatonic University's archaeology teams had spent extensive time in Egypt and the Valley of the Kings as well as the lesser known, and often whispered about, Valley of the Pit, which harbored the secret occult communities that went vastly ignored by the higher classes of Egyptian history. While artifacts from the Valley of the Pit were on display, I had recommended that we not do anything to highlight them nearly as much as the things people expected to find in an Egyptian museum. Much like the Iroquois dream bowl, we hid the related artifacts of the Valley with the rest. It was one thing to invite people to explore history and another to invite people to explore the darkest sides of the occult.

The rest of Carter Hall was filled with the kinds of things

that you would expect to see in an Egyptian wing at a university museum. There were x-rays of sarcophagi, photographs of excavations, murals in the middle of restoration, statues of goats, idols to gods, and a mix of weaponry, farm tools, and instruments from the time period.

The doors to the wing were wide open. We ran through them as a group and halted just as cohesively.

We had walked into another battlefield, courtesy of Icthosthau. Students and faculty were being tossed around the wing with incredible force. The injured littered the floor and if they were still conscious, the assaults didn't stop. We could each see the faint outlines of everyone's own personal nightmares fighting them.

"What now?" Neil asked.

"We sneak past them, right?" Nancy suggested.

I shook my head. "We need something from here first." Pointing at the display on the far-right side of the room, I added, "The sistrum."

Their blank looks reminded me that I wasn't dealing with scholars versed in Ancient Egypt.

"The looped rattle with hooks through its wide bit," I explained. "It's traditionally known as an instrument of the goddess, Bast. That one isn't, though. That one will give us an edge against Icthosthau."

"Get the rattle. Got it," Nancy confirmed before looking down at her arms and gasping. "What's happening?"

It wasn't only happening to her. I saw as outlines of creatures entirely alien to this realm of reality formed themselves around us. A chill filled my stomach as I figured out what was happening.

I looked up and saw that all of the ghostly nightmares of the room had vanished and the only remaining outlines of nightmare flesh were surrounding Sergeant Neil, Nancy, and myself.

"Oh no," Neil said as he reached the same conclusion.

"What?" Fear filled Nancy's voice. "What's going on?"

All of the students and faculty in the Carter Hall turned toward us; rage and terror filled every one of their faces.

All of us were struggling with the moral dilemma of raising our guns and defending ourselves. I could have thrown up a barrier if I still had access to the veil magic. Without it, we were stuck with Icthosthau's clever means of getting around our ash and blood protections.

Nancy was the first of us to flick on her safety and flip her gun to her back by way of the strap. The sergeant and I both holstered our pistols and prepared ourselves in similar fighting stances.

"Try not to hurt them," I suggested before tossing a glance at Nancy, "but don't let them hurt you."

"We'll take the brunt of them," Neil told me. "You get that rattle." He cast a quick smirk toward my friend. "You think you can handle that?"

Nancy returned the smirk, "Better than you, old man."

"I have no doubt." He let out a yell and ran at the students.

Nancy followed, as did I, but I chose to feint at the last second and dove under a slower professor who lunged for me. I briefly recognized her as Judith Funston, the English professor. While I hadn't spoken to her at all in my time as Dean, my time as a student at Miskatonic University had taught me to avoid crossing her. As I avoided her attack, I wasn't sure what I had been afraid of in those days.

I came up into a fighting stance and facing Judith. She swung at me and I moved to block with my new arm and was surprised to find that a student had grabbed it.

"Kill it, Doc," the young lady shouted. My other arm was grabbed by another student the moment I attempted to use it. I had no time to evaluate my next move before Professor Funston let loose a fury of blows to my ribs. Her punches walked up my torso until she was connecting with my chin and if I had been watching from the sidelines, I would have found it almost humorous. Judith was only about half of my height and weighed less than Nancy. Terror had turned her into a force to be reckoned with.

It stands to reason that if you die, meet an all-powerful being, are resurrected, and are generally better for it that you wouldn't have much room in your head for silly things like a fear of dying. In my own case, the exact opposite was true. We spend most of our lives, whether we admit it or not, proving to ourselves that we are invincible. Every small thing we survive only serves as evidence that the world not only revolves around our existence, but that it would also do anything to keep that existence going. Logically, that's completely false, but our minds use that so that we aren't afraid to get into a car, cross the street, or swim in the ocean. We need that lie so that we can live our lives to the fullest. Having lost my life and made a deal with an unreliable and untrustworthy deity, I was now stripped of that fake belief and surrounded by the naked truth.

I could die. It would hurt. The next death would likely be my last.

Something about this revelation while two students pinned me in place and let the elderly Judith Funston punch me over and over again before picking up an Egyptian spear and preparing to run me through awoke something inside of me. The revelation provided the emotional energy to charge up whatever had become of my revived flesh.

With little effort, I threw the students into Professor Funston and the resulting crash sent all three of them hurtling through the display where the professor had retrieved the spear. I wanted to analyze what had happened and understand if the Green Lazarus had augmented my own adrenaline, or if something more mystical and tied to my new connection to Nyarlathotep had been activated.

I had no time for that, though, and needed to get to the sistrum.

Twisting toward my objective, I only barely saw the royal dagger coming toward my face in time to avoid it. The rust-covered glint of dark metal startled me enough that I jumped just out of range of the swing. The young man brandishing it was crying as he screamed and lunged again.

It took little effort for me to disarm and toss him into the Funston pile. Taking the dagger, I threw it skyward and let it embed itself out of everyone's reach in the ceiling.

Two more students came running in my direction and I tried a new tactic. Spreading my arms wide, I roared at the top of my lungs. Everyone in the room froze, including Nancy and Harvey. The museum visitors were seeing whatever terrifying image their minds had given them letting out a bestial wail, while my companions were taking the moment to assess each other's situation.

This gave me a quick glimpse to check on Nancy who was behind a large man with her arm pulled tight around his neck. While she looked at me, he passed out and she let him fall.

Sergeant Neil was overwhelmed by four attackers that Nancy was suddenly free to help even the odds with. Two quick swings with the butt of her gun freed the sergeant enough that he could dispatch the third while Nancy took on the fourth. In everyone's stillness and fear, the smell of sweat and urine hit my nose and I again felt sympathy for the students and staff of Miskatonic University. If I hadn't brought the scroll back to our campus, they wouldn't have had their nightmares thrown at them in this way.

There was nothing graceful in how I broke through the case holding the sistrum. I slammed my shoulder into the glass. Instead of the glass breaking under the impact, the case rocked back and hit the wall. The entire back side of the display shattered. Grabbing the side of the display, I pulled it forward and let it slam into the ground. While it pained me to see all the damage we were doing to these priceless works of history, it would pain me more if we all died.

The sistrum fit nicely in my belt. Everyone in the room was still frozen and not sure what to do. Why weren't the monsters attacking? Why did they hate that one display case so much? Why were they suddenly leaving out the far door and deeper into the museum?

We slammed the doors shut behind us and I stepped back to let the sergeant drag some chairs over. We didn't expect them to come after the monsters who just left the room without killing any of them unless Icthosthau decided to make us look like large bowls of ice cream or something else desirable. Just in case, though, having those chairs blocking the doors wouldn't hurt.

"We got your damn rattle," Neil stated. "Now what?"

"Now," I couldn't hide my excitement that this idea might work and flashed my teeth in a big smile, "we call for reinforcements."

"Reinforcements?" Nancy asked.

I nodded. "I have a theory about how Itchy's powers work. I don't think these projections he's pulling are directly from our minds. He might get the ideas from some sort of psychic impression he gets from us, but the forms and substance have to come from somewhere."

"Hyperborea, right?" Neil guessed.

"No," I answered. "Hyperborea is where he gets his magic to call on these things. To have solidity and substance they have to actually come from somewhere."

"But they aren't actually real," Nancy countered. "These things disappear, and we can filter them out with your weird stars on our foreheads."

"We've just been filtering out our mutual perceptions of the creatures and when they disappear, they go back home. They're real, Nancy, just not real here."

"Alright," Neil barked, "stop with the suspense and tell us where they come from, then."

Nancy figured it out before I could explain.

"The Dream Lands."

"I thought you said that you can't use magic anymore, Doran?" Neil's face was looking more tired as the day progressed. None of us had really rested, aside from my dance with death, since Carol went wild in the armory. To be honest, I hoped I looked half as energetic as Nancy was somehow remaining.

"I can't." Holding up the sistrum, I shook it. "That's why I needed this."

Instead of the rattle of metal on metal that my companions expected from the instrument, a deep hum resonated in our minds and drowned out any other sounds as it bounced around inside our heads.

While it was still ringing, I shouted, "If you needed a damned invitation, this is it."

Sergeant Neil and Nancy spun in place, looking everywhere for our reinforcements to arrive.

"Where the hell are they?" the sergeant demanded.

I saw the outline only faintly and remembered that I was going to have to undo our protections if I was going to see my plan realized. Wiping the Elder Sign off of my forehead, he snapped into focus.

Nancy did the same thing and when Neil noticed the faint ghostly shape, so did he.

I pulled my friend into a tight embrace before he pulled back and looked me up and down.

In a thick French accent, he said, "What have you done to yourself, American?" He inspected my new arm. "And which graves have you been robbing, eh?"

"It's a long story," I said, "and we don't have time to tell it."

"Oui," he agreed. "This is quite the shit show."

"Leo," Nancy shouted before giving him a bear hug.

He grunted with surprise and then gave me a wink as he said to her. "I am glad that you are still around, Miss Dyer. Keeping Andrew barely alive, I see."

"That would be his doing," Nancy pointed at the sergeant.

"Sergeant Harvey Neil," I said as way of introduction, "this is—"

The sergeant thrust out his hand and shook Leo's with a strong grip.

"Leo DuBois," Neil interrupted my introduction. "Formerly of the French Resistance and recently passed while on an excursion with you to Antarctica. Glad to have a real soldier in the mix, son."

"Recently?" Leo furrowed his brow. "Time is different in the Dream Lands."

I nodded, "It's only been a few months."

"Of course," he laughed. "How could it possibly be relaxing around here for more than a few months?"

"If that device," Nancy said, "the sistrum, could bring him back at any time why didn't you use it months ago?"

"It can't bring him back," I answered. "The pharaohs used this sistrum to reach beyond the veil and communicate with other worlds. All I did was let Leo know that we needed him."

"Oui," Leo agreed. "There is, for lack of a better word, a

tunnel between our worlds and Icthosthau is the guardian."
He smirked. "I had to hitch a ride here on one of his other
nightmares. His power drags the beasts of Dream here against
their will; he was not watching for someone to go willingly."

"Leo is made of the same stuff that these unstoppable things
are made of," I added. "He's not flesh like we are."

"A homunculus," Neil understood. "Just an avatar in our
world." He drew his pistol. "Did you come armed?"

Leo smirked and pulled a large machine gun from thin air.
"I am a denizen of Dream, now. I bring anything I need with
me."

"Unfortunately," I said, needing to set expectations for Nancy
and especially myself so that I didn't get too comfortable with
the situation, "once Icthosthau is defeated and his nightmares
go away, so does Leo."

"Back home, I hope," Neil said.

Leo nodded. "If he discovers I am one of his own creations,
he can dismiss me easily enough, but if he does not, then I am
here until the very end."

"Wonderful." I took off down the hall in the general direction
I was hoping we would find Icthosthau. "Then let's move."

Big Dreams

The next set of double doors were wide open. Unlike the other rooms we had entered there wasn't any group of attackers, flesh-beasts, students, or grumpy professors attacking us. Instead of an assault or even the expected room for artifacts from the Roman Empire, there was a room from an alien realm.

The nightmare could have been chosen from any of us just by the sheer size. While I couldn't speak to what Sergeant Neil had seen in his life, I knew that my friends and I had seen places this vast in Antarctica. I had no doubts that the sergeant had dealt with an alien city or two in his life. This could even be something from maybe someone else on campus, or perhaps Icthosthau was digging deep into the recesses of his own ancient memory and pulling something from a long dead person's nightmares. His abilities seemed only limited by the imagination of the people whose universe he was in.

The room before us stood over a mile high. Walls that had no seams or blemishes stretched toward a ceiling that was the same color and I assumed matched in lack of edges or markings. I might have been a healthy man, but even my eyes couldn't make out details that far away. Light filled the entire space but didn't have a source. The air felt charged with some sort of static and as we stepped across the threshold, it was obvious that we weren't the only people there.

At the far end of the room was a large door that seemed proportionate for the size of the room. Stepping out of that door were two beings shaped much as we were with arms and legs and a head. They were completely naked and smooth from head to toe with no eyes, ears, nose, or reproductive organs.

There was nothing to distinguish their gender and they were seemingly identical. Their only identifying feature was a large hole in the middle of their chests filled with teeth.

"Those teeth have to be as large as we are." Nancy's words came out in a hiss of air and fear.

Neil didn't sound any less afraid. "How the hell do we get past them?"

"I don't even know if that's what we want to do," I answered.

"Don't be silly, American." Leo wasn't lowering his voice at all and earned a look from each of us. "We just found the biggest nightmare in this place and you don't think that this is the right direction to find your nightmare god? *Mon dieu*, how did you ever make it all the way to Berlin?"

"Well, some of us have actually died and weren't just shunted to another reality," I countered. "Some of us like the idea of not dying again."

Leo stepped forward and started shooting at the giant monsters. Over his shoulder he shouted, "Your students don't have time for your insecurities."

Nancy looked at me, smirking. I drew my pistol and gave her and Neil a look before saying, "He's talking to all of us." That seemed to snap them from their reflection, and we all opened fire on the monsters and marched forward.

As we caught up to Leo, I asked, "Why was shooting them your plan? Sneaking probably would have worked."

Leo smirked, "Oh yes, they have no eyes." He shrugged. "My apologies. I have had no reason to shoot anything in a long time. I was excited."

I returned my friend's smile, happy to be by his side and fighting again. No, that wasn't all of it. I felt complete for the first time since Antarctica with my friend on my left and my newest friend, and potentially more, on my right. In an odd way, it felt as if the world, or worlds, had been taking things from me for so long that it was a different and welcome feeling of relief when I was able to get something back. Even for as short a time as this was looking to be.

The soldier, just a little further to our right, also seemed to be enjoying the moment as he laughed and reloaded his gun.

The gigantic foreigners to our reality weren't bothered by the bullets but had taken notice of the mice that had decided to throw them at them. They closed on us, but they moved slower than we gave them credit for. First, they tried to stomp on us. The combination of their lack of vision and their slow movements made it easy to avoid their feet. We continued to shoot at them and some of our bullets struck the teeth-like structures in their mouths. That was when we noticed that those structures moved in an odd manner. As the bullets hit them and they quivered, that shake traveled through their entire bodies.

The shaking flesh surged to the edge of their limbs before returning back to their center mass. It all reminded me of gelatin as the waves rocked back toward that center maw.

Once they reached it, each of the teeth vibrated harder and a sound started to fill our ears that we could feel in our bones. Neil, Nancy, and I dropped to our knees and clutched our ears while the monsters screamed louder and louder.

Leo didn't have eardrums or bones by our reality's definition and seemed otherwise unaffected. Seeing us in distress, Leo frowned and then turned back toward the monsters.

His mouth moved and I couldn't hear what was said, but I had no doubts that he was throwing down a gauntlet.

His size increased almost instantly until he was the same size as our two aggressors. He shoved his machine gun into the mouth of one and then his fist into the mouth of the other.

The sound stopped and we could hear his booming voice over the ringing in our ears as we climbed back to our feet.

"I need this more than you do."

Both of the monsters exploded. Gore briefly covered everything before evaporating. In the blink of an eye, Leo was standing beside us and his original size again.

"What did you just do?" Nancy asked him.

"Dreams are just ideas without limits," Leo explained. "I exercised that lack of limits." He shrugged. "If they can be big, I can be big." He shook his head. "That's the wrong question."

"What's the right question?" I was suddenly curious what Leo was having difficulty telling us.

"What makes these nightmares so strong?" He smiled as he asked us.

Sergeant Neil didn't hesitate to answer. "How afraid of them we are?"

"Exactly." Leo clapped Neil on the shoulder. "They are as powerful as we let them be. Well," my friend corrected, "as powerful as you let them be. With you three out of the fight, all I needed to do was steal the energy that was holding their bodies together."

"How does that help you?" I asked.

"I do not know," he gave as an answer, "but perhaps it will make me stronger in the next fight."

"We can use that," Neil said. "Can we get you more of these things to, uh, absorb?"

Leo shrugged. "Don't worry about me. I only just realized that I could do this. It might be nothing."

"Or it might be an edge we can use," I suggested. "Let's keep moving. To your earlier point," I nodded to Leo, "we need to keep moving."

We finished collecting ourselves and closed the distance to the oversized door and ran through it.

And into a blizzard.

The next place we stepped into was a tundra. There was light snow on the ground with dried and dead plant life scattered across the horizon as far as the eye could see. The cold bit through our inadequate clothing and seemed to cut to our bones. It was made all the worse by the forceful winds tearing at us.

We stepped back into the previous room and looked through the door to see where our next destination might be.

"This is the right place," I said. "He's turned it into what he's comfortable with; something that looks like Hyperborea."

"Freezing cold and horrible weather?" Nancy said. "Or he's tapped into my nightmare."

"No, that's his home," I said. "We're close."

The USEC sergeant had pulled binoculars from his pouch and was scanning the scene before us.

"There's something happening on that low mountain." He

pointed at the nearby peak. Halfway up was a congregation of beings all facing a raised throne.

My eyesight hadn't miraculously gotten a thousand times better when I had been resurrected, but I had no doubts that the being on the throne was Icthosthau.

"It's going to be a hike," Nancy said. "We should plan what to do before we get there."

We all agreed and set about preparing for what we expected to be our final assault on the prisoner god. We communicated what we hoped would be a winning strategy and then we began reloading and checking over our weapons. We stretched our limited out-of-season clothing to cover as much of our exposed skin as we could. Once we were as prepared as we could possibly hope to be, we stepped again through the doorway and into the winter nightmare.

The Winter Nightmare

When we had previously stepped through the door and into the nightmare visage of Hyperborea, we had been a mile from the mountain that Neil had seen Icthosthau on.

As we stepped through it this second time, we were on the mountain and directly behind the throng of worshipers bent in submission to the prisoner god's throne. We weren't cold any longer, either. It was as if we were still standing in the museum.

The people between us and the throne were about a thousand deep with a part in the center that allowed for a direct path to the throne. They were mostly humans dressed in tribal furs and with looks of terror in their eyes. The rest were close to human and of varying bipedal species that I mostly didn't recognize. They were clearly intelligent and native to Hyperborea, and carried the same heavy looks of terror that their human counterparts did.

The throne at the end of the path stood almost ten feet high and was made of antlers, bone, and wood. It was held together by lichen and moss with patches of frozen mud. Just as we had suspected, sitting on the throne was Icthosthau as I had last seen him.

He was dressed all in furs with leather bands tying them to his body. His shape was that of the traditional mountain man with a thick beard to his chest and more furs as a hat. He chewed on a hunk of meat that was still dripping blood.

After the initial shock of the situation had subsided, I started marching up the path toward the throne. My companions followed closely behind me. None of us took our eyes from Icthosthau as he began clapping, heralding our approach.

"For humans, you have shown yourself to be quite incredible." His voice boomed and carried through the entire world. "And your Dream Land friend? That was very clever, calling on help with my own powers." He stopped clapping and took another bite from the meat he was still holding. "I do wonder what it is that you hoped to accomplish."

I stopped in front of Icthosthau while my friends started to spread out.

"I want you off of my campus and gone from my world." My tone was conversational, but there was enough volume for anyone there to hear.

"We are not on your world anymore." He swam his finger through the air in the path of a star. "Draw your Elder Sign again and take a look." He spread his arms wide. "I am a god. I created a portal between our worlds. It doesn't matter what world I'm in anymore."

I now understood and sympathized with the fear of his audience. They were the actual people of Hyperborea brought low by the return of their demon. They had thought the nightmare god, Icthosthau had been forever cast away to never harm them again. Then some dumb archaeologist in another realm of existence had decided to upset the balance that kept the prisoner god locked away.

"But Hyperborea is your source," I asked, "your home?"

Icthosthau's lips curled into a sinister grin. "If I was a clever man, I would call it your grave, but I thought I had already killed you." He shrugged. "Omnipotence isn't what it used to be."

It was my turn to smile. "I get that a lot." My fingers were itching to hold my sword, but that wasn't ever going to happen again. I knew my friends were desperate to shoot him, but we each had a part to play and I needed to play mine.

"What do I need to do to convince you to leave Earth alone?" It was an honest enough question, but even I couldn't hide the derision from my voice.

"Poor, deluded, food." His voice was filled with pity. "How could I possibly give up your beautiful world?" Icthosthau stood from his throne. "I was born of this world from the nightmares that only the cold winds of Ithaqua could create in the huddled and starving people of the caves. They are so few, and their horrifying scraps fed me, nurtured me, and starved me into existence." He wiped his mouth; spittle flew as he spoke. "Then Eibon showed me your succulent world with its people filling every corner, to the brim, with its dark nightmares of worlds and scenes I would never have access to. I could hear the echoes of horrors that Elder Gods would dream in resolute passing while your people echoed them, changed them, shifted them into newer and worse creations. I could feed and get fat from your world. My power would be unlimited." His eyes lit with an icy blue light and he bellowed his next words. "And then Eibon locked me away."

His people, if that was what you called subjugated people forced into worshiping a devil, let out a moan at the mention of the wizard's name.

Sergeant Neil had pulled out the wooden dream bowl and was scraping the insides of it. Once his finger was covered in enough ash and blood mixture, he reached up to his forehead and tried to draw the Elder Sign as he could remember it. He only got the first dried-out line on his head when Icthosthau waved his hand. The Iroqouis artifact ignited and turned to ash almost instantly.

While Icthosthau was admiring his handiwork and Neil was jumping back from the flaming artifact, the rest of us opened fire.

I was rewarded with the telltale sizzle and rotting flesh when my pistol, which Nancy had called Elliot Ness's Equalizer, finally hit an otherworldly monster with its magicked bullets. Icthosthau roared and leapt toward me. The flesh dropped from his body as my bullets hit him, but Nancy's bullets had the same effect.

When we had taken the time to prepare, we applied the lessons we had learned toward a strategy that had the best chance of taking down this Hyperborean god. We used the last of the blood Carol had loaned us in Leo's old flask, and soaked our bullets in the bowl. Nancy had pocketed more of those brochures, so we had filled the bowl with ash and blood and armed ourselves with explosive tokens that could filter the dream effect. If his power was dreams, we would hurt the dreams.

Every time that a piece of Icthosthau's flesh would fall, the blackened bones and gray flesh of his real form became visible. By the time he had reached me, his body was an unmatching conglomeration of human form contorted by the larger flesh of an alien god. His head was half antlered corpse with glowing red eyes and one arm had grown in length to accommodate the larger forearm of blackened bone. Even hurting him was creating a nightmare beast that was somehow worse than either of his forms by itself.

He swung at Nancy first. She had run at us as he stomped toward me and she was obviously afraid of losing me again. Nancy blocked with her tommy gun, but the sheer force of being punched by a god sent her flying away from the mountain.

In anger or fear, I wasn't certain, I charged the demon.

From the corner of my eye I saw Leo, with powers that could only have been borrowed by his existence as a dream creature, suddenly appear in the air and catch Nancy before bringing her back to the ground near us.

I let my relief distract me and my charge was interrupted by a backhand from Icthosthau that I didn't see coming.

My hand shot up and caught the prisoner god's swing by the forearm and stopped its forward momentum entirely.

No, not my arm.

Private Tim Ruddel's arm.

I didn't know if it was Ruddel's spirit or Nyarlathotep's dirty work from the piece of himself he had put where Olivia had once been, but in that moment I was grateful.

Icthosthau was not.

His eyes went wide with a mix of rage and confusion. How had this mortal survived his first death at the hands of this god? How could this powerless thing of flesh halt a god's attack?

They were good questions, and if I wasn't the one benefiting from the results, I would have been asking them too.

I twisted his arm away from me and brought my pistol into his chest and pulled the trigger. He howled and hit me with both arms, and I expected to fly off of the mountain as Nancy had.

Instead, his subjugated worshipers, who had just seen me stand up to him, caught me and brought me back to the path that had led to the throne.

Betrayal joined the rage and confusion on Icthosthau's face.

A black mist began to coalesce directly between myself and Icthosthau, and I noticed his hands were twisting as it appeared. A beast twice my size, with flowing black robes containing mounds upon mounds of squirming black tentacles covered in tiny mouths, took form.

"It would seem that you did more than come back to life," Icthosthau stated. His voice was becoming less human and more like stone grinding against stone. "It seems you brought back new nightmares as well."

He was right. My biggest fear was losing control of myself in my quest to protect the world. I had faced it in my original nightmare vision of the Bringer of Cthulhu, and I had faced it over and over again in my confrontations with the psychic parasite that was Olivia. Those were byproducts of my dabbling in the arcane forces from beyond the veil and they hadn't happened to me so much as they had been a promise to happen to me.

That fear had changed to a reality when Nyarlathotep had brought me back to life. When he had put a piece of himself inside of me and labeled me one of his agents here on Earth, he had accomplished what none of the other nightmares had.

He succeeded.

I was no longer in control of my destiny. It was a trade that I had been willing to make for the continued success of the human race, but it had meant giving up any control of my future. If Nyarlathotep's plan for me was to turn me into the next monster or to have me ruling the world there was little that I would be able to do about it. I could only hope that he either had more altruistic plans for myself, which was unlikely, or that I would be able to outsmart an omniscient god. And Nyarlathotep's omniscience was arguably more all-seeing than any of the other monsters that claimed the power, for he was their messenger. He was the chaos that delivered the information to each of them. He might not be the strongest, but he had the most knowledge, and that was his true power.

And that was why the beast from my nightmares stood before me. It was Nyarlathotep made flesh in the common form that many associated with him except for one small difference. My face was swimming across one of his alien tentacles.

"I feel it." Icthosthau was growing his flesh back and beginning to look human again, even though my companions hadn't stopped shooting him with our dream-defeating bullets. "Your fear is fresh and new. Like an apple picked right off the branch."

"Good," I said through the gritted teeth of my terror. Nyarlathotep was gliding toward me. His tentacles were reaching out to collect me and pull me inside.

Icthosthau hadn't heard my answer over his lust for my fear. If he had, he might have asked why it was a good thing that I was feeding him more of the power that he craved.

Part of our strategy involved giving Icthosthau our most powerful fears. First, Nancy tried to defend me, and the god attacked her. That fear lanced through me quickly but it obviously gave him strength. Leo had intercepted that flow of power and used it to save her. That had tested our plan.

Then I opened my mind as much as someone who had spent their formative years learning to block out penetrating spells could. I thought hard on what scared me the most. About losing myself to my new role and being the one who brought about the same end of the world that I had fought so hard to stop.

Icthosthau had gobbled that right up.

Leo leapt on Nyarlathotep.

The prisoner god was too lost in his feast to notice that my friend had been inching closer this entire time. Nyarlathotep reacted as any of the aggressive nightmares had before and turned to take on the new attacker. Leo was fighting multiple limbs at once and his own attention must have slipped as three and then four arms of his own came from nowhere and helped grapple with the gnashing tentacles.

The people of Hyperborea weren't just sitting by anymore. They had seen their tormenter challenged and had no desire to go back to living in fear like their ancestors. As one, they swarmed the fake Nyarlathotep. They were tossed and bitten by his many tentacles and mouths, but this projection wasn't the real thing. Finally, Leo shoved his fist into the largest mouth, contained within a tentacle that was under the hood of the robe, and Nyarlathotep exploded.

All of the Hyperborean people and Leo fell to the ground, but Leo wasn't going to rest. He dove at Icthosthau and grappled with the demon.

None of us could afford a moment to rest and we knew it.

Leo was the first to move, tackling Icthosthau and grappling him to the ground. They wrestled for a bit before Leo had the prisoner god from behind with his arms wrapped around Itchy's from the bottom and his legs around Itchy's waist.

All of the power that Leo had absorbed from my terrifying fear, along with the energies he had absorbed from the giants previously, gave him enough of Icthosthau's own strength to pin him down.

Or so we hoped.

Leo's strength seemed to be enough at the moment as Icthosthau transformed into his true shape of blackened bone and oddly shaped tiger and deer head.

Just to be certain, we had put an Elder Sign on a strip of cloth ripped from Nancy's sleeve and drawn in the same ash and blood mixture we had put on our bullets. As soon as Leo had the Icthosthau pinned, she ran up behind him and pressed the still damp symbol to his head. She tied the sleeve strip onto his head like a bandana and stepped back.

That was when Sergeant Neil had tossed me his knife. I caught it in a midair leap and landed on Icthosthau's chest.

And I began carving.

As the knife sliced through the demon flesh of his chest, black blood oozed out from beneath it. I tried to draw the symbol from memory, but it wasn't as easy as I had hoped.

Icthosthau slowed his struggle and began twisting his hands and chanting some sort of Hyperborean spell. Nightmares showed up in the form of more of his flesh-beasts and newer squid-like things that could fly, but they were faint ghosts as the symbol pressed to his head filtered his dream magic. They tried to pull us away, but nothing happened.

That was when we noticed Icthosthau struggling more and I saw that Leo's form had faded a bit as well. If not for the extra power he had absorbed he would already have been useless. We needed to work faster.

Icthosthau's chant grew louder and we could all feel a pressure change in the air. We felt multiple bursts as our ears popped first once, then three and then four times in succession.

Neil shoved his gun into Itchy's face. "What was that?"

The prisoner god's monstrous face shifted into what I assumed was a smile before speaking in a voice that resonated in our souls. "I am closing your doors."

"Doors?" Neil asked, and then recognition appeared on his face. "You're closing the gates between our worlds?"

"If I am to live here diminished," the beast snickered, "I shall not do so alone."

Finishing up the symbol as best I could, I nodded to Leo and fell back from the monster.

Icthosthau shrugged Leo off and stood in all of his horrifying glory before us. Except he was wearing the symbol that the Traum Kultist had taught me to limit Carol's connection to Hyperborea. He still had his powers but now it should only be about as strong as when he had been in the scroll.

Admittedly, that wasn't perfect, either. When he had only been locked in Eibon's scroll prison he could still manipulate us to think that a thousand undead monsters were attacking the campus, but that was only a handful of us and not the entire campus.

Which meant that as long as he stayed in Hyperborea, Earth would be safe.

"One gate left," his voice came out as a bellow and I had no idea whether that was intentional or just a part of who the demon beast spoke in his uglier form. "Can you guess which one?"

He tore off the bandana on his head and wiped away the residual ash and blood. It was obviously helpful, as Leo came back into existence. Icthosthau turned his attention to Leo.

Leo gave me a quick salute and shot Nancy a wink.

"I tire of you," Icthosthau said.

Leo vanished. Returned, I hoped, to his home and life in the Dream Lands.

"We need to get to that portal," I shouted to Nancy.

Before she could verbalize her agreement, Icthosthau took off running down the mountainside at a great speed.

In all our strategizing, we hadn't planned on Icthosthau immigrating to our world and I had no idea how we were going to stop the monster.

Without thinking about it, I took after the demon god. I raced down the hill as quickly as I could and was surprised to see myself gaining on him. Something inside of me that sounded much more reasonable that I felt at that moment told me that this wasn't normal. I ignored that voice as I hunched over and ran. My blood seemed to sing to me, and I could feel energy almost radiating from it. I might not have the powers of the void, but my resurrection seemed to have granted me a strength I had yet to explore.

I leapt onto the back of Icthosthau like a wild cat attacking a gazelle. My teeth sunk into what little flesh coated his neck and I didn't taste anything except for desire.

The desire for this prey to die.

It was obvious, when I looked back at this moment, that the Green Lazarus serum and the insanity that had been known to make its subjects more bestial was trying to do the same to me. It was only in that moment, when I heard Nancy's voice shouting to hurry, that I was able to bring myself back under control.

Nancy and the sergeant were running up behind us, having finally caught the racing demon god and his pursuing undead dean.

I jumped off of Icthosthau and landed to his side. He swung at me and missed before he started running again at the portal. The portal just stood there mocking us, only a couple dozen feet away. It floated in the middle of the great tundra. On our side an entire world, on the other side a campus that was, hopefully, tending to its wounded.

He hadn't made it a step before my new arm shot out and grabbed Icthosthau's black bone wrist and yanked him back toward me and to the ground at my feet. He landed hard just as Nancy and Neil ran by.

Nancy stopped and grabbed my hand.

"Go," I said. "I've got to stop him and then I'll be right behind you."

She looked concerned as though I might be lying, but I wasn't. I didn't want to die on Hyperborea, but I needed to make sure that Icthosthau wasn't going to come after us.

She seemed to see that in my eyes and took off for the gate.

Icthosthau moved to get up but I kicked him back down. His hand began twisting in the same way that it had when we were holding him down earlier and I knew he was trying to close this gate.

The edges began to fade, and it flickered just as Nancy and the sergeant jumped through.

I stomped down on his hand and the spell stopped but the damage was done. The portal was going to close.

I grabbed his throat with my original hand and used my newly donated hand to punch down. My fist went through his skull and into whatever the black mess was that Icthosthau used as a brain.

Icthosthau wasn't a physical entity in the way people were. My damage wouldn't stop him, only slow him down, but that was all I needed. As the prisoner god writhed on the ground I turned and sprinted for the gate.

I leapt through as it was still flickering and was grateful to be back in my museum with my friends, even if that meant without Leo. He was back in his home and I couldn't ask for anything better than that.

Before I had caught my breath, it was gone again as Nancy's mouth crashed into mine. We kissed and held each other for what felt like a long time while the sergeant laughed and fell against the wall.

The portal continued to flicker, faltering and disappearing for longer lengths of time until I thought that it was done and sealed.

That was my mistake.

"I can't believe that we did it," Nancy exclaimed.

The portal flickered open. A broken wrist made of black bone and one still intact with long black phalanges stretched through and grabbed Nancy.

She grabbed the shelf by the portal and fought with all of her strength against the broken nightmare god. I leapt forward to grab her, knowing that together our strength could save her.

I jerked to a stop as something caught my arm.

No. My arm had caught something.

I looked back and the arm that had been grafted to my body had found purchase on a bolted display case. Every command that I sent to it was ignored. Every effort to pull myself or the display case free was worthless.

Then, as a gift or perhaps a moment of torture, a wall came down between the two ideas I should have combined long ago.

Nyarlathotep had first introduced himself to me in the Dream Lands as Timothy. When I had died, he had filled a piece of my broken soul with a part of himself to claim me and make me whole. When I had been resurrected, they had used Timothy Ruddel's arm to complete me.

Timothy Ruddel was Nyarlathotep in this world.

He always had been.

This was the first demand he made of me and I was helpless to resist as the shattered remains of the ancient deity pulled the woman I loved through a portal and into Hyperborea.

The final gate between our worlds closed.

One Week Later

The campus was referring to the entire incident as a gas leak from a mining effort in the Blasted Heath, not far from here. Supposedly, a cloud of·different gasses had escaped from the ground and floated over the campus, causing brief hysteria that led to injury and four deaths on the campus.

Including that of Nancy Dyer, the daughter of respected former professor, William Dyer, and my personal assistant.

Sergeant Harvey Neil needed to get back to the people who commanded him and let them know what happened here and what had happened to his men. Mostly he needed to inform them that the Scroll of Eibon was neutralized and that Jack had been a horrible mistake.

He thanked me for my assistance and offered me condolences on Nancy. We both know that she isn't dead, but with all of the gates between our worlds closed there was no immediate way to find her. Even knowing that, he promised to look for gates that Icthosthau might have missed. He would send me any information if there was even a hint of information about Hyperborea.

Carol and I had a slightly harder time getting back to work. I didn't want to think about anything except getting back to Nancy, and Carol didn't know how to field the influx of requests for my attention from the parents of the injured or deceased or from the faculty or from just about everyone in the world who wanted to know what had actually happened.

As for the Traum Kult, or whatever they were calling themselves now, we hadn't heard a single thing from them since the portal closed and the campus returned, more or less, to normal.

The sergeant had also left me with a gift, of sorts. I was now the proud caretaker of the Mi-Go brain cylinder and Jack was my personal assistant and repository of all things esoteric. Having no body increased his recall capacity. With his research and background with the United States Esoteric Cavalry, he was my new best resource for just about anything that went bump in the night.

Then there was today's letter.

The Board of Directors had sent over a letter.

Dr. Andrew Doran,

In light of the situation on campus and your direct connection to it and the solution, we find ourselves the custodians of an unfortunate decision.

You are to be removed as Dean of Miskatonic University.

We are an informed group and are not unaware of your efforts on behalf of this school and its people. We do not make this decision lightly but find it necessary to save face. We hope that this does not discourage you from continuing your efforts. Please know that while you are no longer the dean, we hope that you will remain available for any classes or expeditions that might require your attention.

There is no doubt that we will need you.

There is also no doubt that we need you to be less in the spotlight case by this prestigious institution.

Good luck in your endeavors and thank you for your service,

The Board of Directors

PS: Your replacement will be coming by to introduce herself to you this afternoon.

That last line had caught me off guard. I had expected them to fire me sooner or later. The part that was surprising was that this very traditional institution had chosen to replace me with a woman. I was impressed with the forward-thinking behavior and only disappointed that it wasn't Carol or Nancy taking that role.

Until she stepped through my door.

Her blond hair was pulled back into a bun. She had dark eyes and high cheekbones and was dressed in a scholarly way. The only indication of who she truly was rested around her neck. She wore a necklace with a pendant that was shaped like a head with an eye in the center of it.

The symbol of the Traum Kult.

"Anita Blumenthal," I spat and drew my pistol as I leapt from my desk.

"Put the gun away, Doran. No one here knows me the way you do." She walked around the office and examined the furniture and bookshelves. "I will be moving in on Monday. Can you be out before the weekend?"

"Excuse me?" I demanded. My gun stayed right where it was.

"I am the new dean." She pointed to the open letter. "I am your replacement."

"Not anymore you aren't," I countered. "The minute I tell them that you're with the Traum Kult they will kick you out of the country."

"No," Anita said, "they won't." She waved her hand around the office. "I don't know if you have noticed, but your reputation took a dive recently. The only highlight that any of them brag about is that you destroyed the Traum Kult." She slowly clapped. "Good job, by the way. Damn those sinners. If you tell them I am with the Traum Kult, it will confuse them, and after that letter, they'll see it as a pitiful attempt to keep your job."

I pointed at her chest where the pendant hung. "I'll show them that."

"This?" She picked it up and held it out to me. "You mean my necklace for my," she snickered as she remembered my own phrasing, "book club?" She let the pendant fall. "This isn't the symbol of the Traum Kult. We're just a group of historically interested readers. You might even want to join us. We call ourselves the Caretakers."

So that was it. They called themselves the Caretakers now and I was in a corner with only my wits and no school support.

Good.

The previous dean had forced me to work with the school and I had been roped into being the new dean when he had died. I had never wanted it or needed it. I wouldn't need it now.

Smiling, I grabbed her hand and shook it vigorously.

"It's a pleasure to finally meet you Miss Blumenthal," I walked her back toward the door. "I'll be out by Friday. I can't wait to see how this role suits you."

I pushed her out the door and shut it behind me. Hopefully, my reaction would make her nervous.

My to-do list was getting a little longer every day.

I still needed to figure out how Nyarlathotep planned to use me, save Nancy from Hyperborea, and now destroy the Caretakers.

Sighing, I looked around the office. It was time to start packing.

Epilogue

I was finally getting somewhere with my packing. So, when I hurried back to my office, rushing past my secretary in the outer office, with an armful of books that I was only borrowing and in no way stealing from my alma mater, I was not too happy finding a second-hand book salesman waiting for me.

His name was Cross. He must have been in his sixties and he looked even more like a hobo than the last time I saw him. He had located some rare volumes for the Miskatonic University Library over the years, and every book came with a long story about how he found it. Today I was not in the mood or position any longer. He should talk to the Library Committee or maybe Miss Blumenthal on Monday.

"Carol!" I shouted. She knew she was not supposed to let people in.

"Andrew—Dr Doran—Dean," said Cross, in his clear British accent. "You're looking awfully well. It's been what, two or three years?"

My secretary did not reply. I was going to have to throw him out myself. I moved forward.

"Sorry not to get up," he said, offering to shake hands. "The foot, you know."

I paused. "Alright, Cross." I said. Some of the irritation had worn off. It was true we had known each other a long time. He was going for the sympathy vote by reminding me he had lost a leg in the Great War; he knew how I would feel if he limped pathetically out.

Mainly it was my rational side kicking in. Cross would not have risked U-Boats and come three thousand miles to see me without a good reason. "Make your pitch. You've got—"I looked at my watch—"three minutes."

Cross smiled at my grouchy tone. "Always rush-rush-rush with you Americans, eh? Still, I think I have something that's worth three minutes of your time."

He rummaged in an old carpetbag and placed a book on my desk. It was a cloth-bound notebook, late nineteenth century, covered in what looked like oil stains. Not exactly the crumbling, millennia-old grimoire he normally showed up with. It didn't look nearly valuable enough to have caught his attention.

"I gather you have acquired a rather special .38 revolver," said Cross. "Perhaps belonging to the famed American, Elliot Ness?"

"So, what if I have?"

He riffled the pages of the book: it was full of hand-drawn diagrams and pages of sparse, spiky text. "This is the field manual for it. Or at least it's the notes left by the chap who made it."

I was mildly curious as to the .38's origin, especially after what Nancy had told me, but I had other things on my mind. "You point it and pull the trigger," I said. "That's about all I need to know."

"Tut, tut, that's no way for a man of learning to talk. And you're supposed to be a dean!" He held up his hands before adding, "Excuse me, 'former Dean.' Mind if I have a look at the weapon in question?"

"Sure," I said, passing it over. "Two minutes left."

Cross turned the gun over, admiring the workmanship. "I'm glad you're looking after it." He flipped open the cylinder and fished out a handful of ammunition from one deep pocket. "But I don't think you've figured out all its wrinkles."

"Those are .45s," I said, "Wrong caliber, they won't go—"

The big bullets fit perfectly. Cross looked up at me, raised his eyebrows, smiled, then flicked the cylinder shut. He flicked it open again and the cylinder was empty, like one of those trick wallets that makes money disappear.

"This revolver has a bigger capacity than you might think," he said.

"So I see," I said.

"It might look like it was made in a factory," he said, loading another six rounds. "But it wasn't. There's a place in the Khyber Pass, Northwest Frontier, where they make perfect copies of guns. Perfect copies. Also, they make outstanding curries if you like a bit of spice. Back in Queen Victoria's day the British couldn't figure out where the tribes were getting all these Martini-Henry rifles from. Then they realized that all the rifles had the same serial number. They were copies."

"Is that where the .38 was made?" I couldn't deny my curiosity was growing.

"Remarkable gunsmith, that chap who made it," he said. "There's a section in the book on care and maintenance you'll need to have a look at. Needs more than a drop of oil now and then. Wouldn't want it to stop working."

"Okay, Cross, I'm interested," I said.

"There's a whole chapter on non-Euclidean ballistics," he said. "I was never any good at geometry at school myself— hypotenuses and whatnot never made any sense to me—but I can do this."

He held his hand up and pointed the gun at it. Before I could stop him, he pulled the trigger. There was a sharp crack, a puff of smoke, and a bullet thudded into the wall. Cross held up his hand, completely undamaged.

"Did that bullet just pass through your hand?"

"Around it, I think," he said. "I told you I couldn't do geometry. You have to adjust the sights, but that's the general idea."

"How much do you want for it?" Cross never gave anything away.

"This book could save your life in a fight," said Cross. "And from what I hear—" he tapped his lips to show that he knew this was secret "—you're in a few of those. This book is worth more than mere money."

It did not take a genius to figure out what he was after. "You want one of the books from our library," I said. "That's what you came here for."

"Before you vacated the premises," he said, leaning forward,

"I thought it might be prudent to ask for a loan of Trithemius Metagraphiae."

The book was an infamous occult work written in alchemical code, undeciphered and probably undecipherable, with a reputation for unleashing hellish forces. Burning brimstone had ripped through more than one scholar's cell while they struggled to decode it, destroying everything except the tome itself. Like the other works from our special collection that book was never allowed to leave the building.

I really wanted the notebook though. Cross was right when he said it could be a big help to me. He was a known, trusted individual, so maybe we could make a special exception... then something occurred to me.

"Wait a minute," I said. There had been a letter from London two weeks ago from the Special Operations Executive, the British military intelligence organization. It was still in my in-box, and I quickly re-read it. "Are you with the SOE? They said they were sending someone about a book."

"I suppose you mean this," Cross grumbled, pulling an ID card from an inner pocket. It showed he had joined the SOE six months earlier, with the rank of Captain.

"Of course we can lend the book out to the British government, if it's needed for the war effort," I said. "Why didn't you tell me that first?"

"I'm a dealer in rare and valuable books," he said. "Not a bloody spy."

"Whatever," I said. I paused and then added. "Given my circumstances and," I lowered my voice, "the situation that is my replacement, perhaps it might go missing before you return it?"

"Ah," he smiled. "You mean the woman with the Traum Kult? I think we might be able to make that happen."

I was relieved to know that the Caretakers wouldn't be getting their hands on at least one dreadful tome. "Cross, we have a deal."

"Splendid! I had better bring your secretary back then."

"Excuse me?"

"I used a small cantrip against wendigo I found on some eighteenth-century wampum to put her out," he said. "That woman is terrifying."

About the Author

Matthew Davenport hails from Des Moines, Iowa where he lives with his wife, Ren, and daughter, Willow. When his scattered author brain isn't earning weird looks from the ladies of his life, he enjoys reading sci-fi and horror, tinkering with electronics, and doing escape rooms.

Matt is the author of the Andrew Doran series, the Broken Nights series (along with his brother, Michael), *The Trials of Obed Marsh*, and *Satan's Salesman* among other titles.

He's also a self-styled student of the Cthulhu Mythos and exercises that influence in his stories and as part-time editor at the blog Shoggoth.net.

You can keep track of Matthew through his Twitter account @spazenport or his blog authormatthewdavenport.wordpress. com.

Novels

Random Stranger
Stranger Books
The Trials of Obed Marsh
The Statement of Andrew Doran
Andrew Doran at the Mountains of Madness
The Sons of Merlin
Broken Nights
Broken Nights: Strange Worlds
Satan's Salesman
Anthologies
Blackest Knights
Somebody, Save Me!: Superheroes and Vile Villains Book 5
Tales of the Al-Azif
Time Loopers
The Book of Yig: Revelations of the Serpent
Tales of Yog-Sothoth

Coming Soon!

Satan's Salesman 2: *The Devil is in the Details*

Curious about other Crossroad Press books?
Stop by our site:
http://store.crossroadpress.com
We offer quality writing
in digital, audio, and print formats.